Into the Shadows

by Karly Kirkpatrick

Copyright © 2010 by Karly Kirkpatrick

This book is a work of fiction. Names, characters, places and incidents are either products of the author's imagination or used fictitiously. Any resemblance to actual events, locales, or persons, living or dead, is entirely coincidental. All rights reserved. No part of this publication can be reproduced or transmitted in any form or by any means, electronic or mechanical, without permission in writing from the author or publisher.

For Annikka Päivi

Chapter One

Sweet Dreams

Five years ago...

Streams of sunlight shone brightly through the car window as shadows of the passing trees flickered across Paivi Anderson's face. Next to her sat a woman she knew well, but as she glanced around she was slightly confused. Looking over her shoulder into the back seat she was surprised to see that Michaela wasn't in the car. Though they had been friends forever it was rare that Paivi was in the car with Michaela's mother by herself. Mrs. Brown, an older version of her daughter and sporting the same long, dark hair, hummed along with a song on the radio. She seemed unaware of Paivi sitting next to her.

In an instant the car slammed to a violent stop and Paivi pitched forward in her seat. Glass shattered—small pieces rained down on her and she could hear the horrible sound of crunching metal. Mrs. Brown screamed as rivers of blood ran down her face, which had been sliced by the flying glass. An oily smoke filled the car, surging through the vents. Paivi's lungs burned as she gasped for air, choking and sputtering. She looked down to see flames licking at her feet from under the dashboard. She was frozen, unable to move as the scorching heat raced up her legs. A deafening explosion shook them, rocking the car.

Paivi screamed and thrashed in pain, trying to free herself from the flaming wreckage tangled around her. She didn't want to open her eyes, terrified of what she would see. Cool hands grasped her arms and in the distance she heard a familiar voice.

"She's having another dream, John!" Mrs. Anderson's voice was panicked as she wrestled with the tangled mass before her.

Paivi opened an eye and saw her room.

"Help me! No, no, no!" she screamed, fighting against the damp sheet that had woven itself around her limbs and clung to her body. Her pajamas were soaked with sweat and she could still feel the heat from the fire, despite being aware she was no longer in it.

Mrs. Anderson frantically attempted to untangle the sheet from around Paivi's thin frame.

"Sweetheart, what's wrong? Are you okay?"

"No, Mom, I don't know, it's Mrs. Brown." Paivi was rambling—unable collect her thoughts. Finally able to sit up, she gulped hungrily at the air, struggling to find her breath. Mrs. Anderson put her arms around Paivi, and smoothed her sweaty hair back from her forehead. "I saw her in my dream. There was some kind of accident. In the car. But I don't think she's okay. You have to do something!" she pleaded.

Mr. and Mrs. Anderson exchange concerned looks.

Into the Shadows

This wasn't the first time their young daughter had experienced such a vivid dream. It became difficult for Mr. and Mrs. Anderson to stop Paivi from making connections as she got older. Her 'dreams' came true all too often. She often shared them with her parents, but she had never envisioned such a tragic event. Mostly they were trivial things, such as finding a lost bike or watching herself earn an A on an upcoming test.

Mr. and Mrs. Anderson supported Paivi's visions and never made her feel different. Little did she know it was because they were comforted by the thought that other adults would merely look upon her as a precocious child with an over-active imagination. This would keep her secret safe from the citizens of St. Andrew, Illinois. Besides, Paivi was, in most respects, a normal little girl from a happy family and that's all anyone really needed to know.

Mrs. Anderson spoke softly, "I don't know if there is much we can do."

"What do you mean Mom? Dad, you're a policeman. Please do something! We have to call them! I have to call Michaela!" Paivi screamed hysterically. She fought against her mom's arms with no success. Mrs. Anderson only held her tighter.

"Paivi, I am so sorry," Mr. Anderson said. "Sometimes we see things we wish we couldn't, but there is nothing we can do. When the time is right, your Mom and I will explain this all to you. But right now you need to trust us. You'll need to be there for Michaela. And you have to promise us that you won't tell anyone about your dream tonight."

Mr. Anderson knelt down beside her and took her hand. Paivi was sobbing so hard that she could not respond. Gulps and shudders were now the only sounds she could manage.

"Okay," she whispered.

Paivi sat up crying for a few more hours before falling asleep, exhausted, in her mother's arms.

Mrs. Anderson called her out of school the next day.

"The library books can wait until tomorrow, I'm sure they don't mind," she said as she pulled a tray of Paivi's favorite chocolate chip cookies out of the oven. "Miss Nelson said she hoped you feel better," she offered, referring to the head librarian at the St. Andrew Public Library, where she worked.

Paivi shoved the cookies away, uninterested.

Everything in the house reminded her of Michaela and Mrs. Brown. Commercials showing a mother and daughter running together in the park and the plot of her mom's soap opera wouldn't allow her to block the thoughts from her mind. She spent most of the day curled up next to her mom on the couch. She shivered as her mom stroked her long, blond hair and held her close, wondering if Michaela would get a chance to do the same with her mom again.

In the afternoon she asked her mom calmly, her green eyes shining with hope, "Mom, are you sure there anything we can do? Can't we call someone?"

"Honey, I promise you, if there was any way to change what you saw, I would do it for you and for Mrs.

Brown. But sometimes there are things we can't change. When you're a little older, you'll understand this better." She attempted a bitter half-smile, which was meant more for herself than for Paivi. Dark circles floated under her sky blue eyes. "Not that it makes it any easier. Just know that you are special and we love you very much."

She kissed Paivi on the head.

And so they waited. Paivi's stomach churned as she thought about having to face Michaela. She was able to dodge her phone call after school but she knew there would be no escaping her the next day.

The phone call came that evening, from Mr. Anderson himself. Mrs. Anderson answered, her voice muted. She turned back to Paivi, who sat anxiously at the kitchen table, shredding a paper napkin.

"That was your Daddy. Mrs. Brown had an accident today. She was taken to St. Andrew Medical. She is still alive, but very badly injured," Mrs. Anderson paused, wiping away a tear as it trickled down her cheek, "they're not sure if she'll make it."

This time Paivi did not cry. Mrs. Brown was alive, and for right now that was enough for her.

Despite the best efforts of her doctors and weeks in the hospital, Mrs. Brown wasn't getting any better. She had been badly burned in the explosion and was forced to endure numerous surgeries. Paivi was unable to avoid Michaela for long, as the Andersons had kindly offered to take care of Michaela and her little sister Marissa while Mr. Brown tended to his ailing wife. At first, things were awkward. Paivi worried that Michaela would somehow figure out the truth—that she had known about the accident. She felt like it was written in red letters across her forehead.

"Paivi," Michaela said one night as she and Paivi settled in for their fourth sleepover that week. She twisted in her sleeping bag and turned towards Paivi, trying to keep from waking Marissa who was asleep at her feet. "I'm scared. I mean, Marissa isn't because she's so little, but I've heard my dad talking on the phone. I don't want my mom to die, Paivi."

Paivi could see her wipe away tears in the light of the night-light. She felt her own eyes overflow; tears spilled silently down her cheeks. She reached out and grabbed Michaela's hand.

"I don't want her to die either," she whispered, wishing that her words were enough to change what she knew would happen.

On a beautiful spring day, Mrs. Brown passed away. Guilt oozed out of every pore as Paivi trudged across the graveyard towards the waiting crowd dressed in black. She clasped her mom's hand, hoping that it would be over quickly. She couldn't bear looking at the life, now over, sitting on the dais in front of them. Michaela had taken it better than Paivi, something that she struggled to comprehend. She wondered how her friend could be so strong.

Paivi returned home after Mrs. Brown's funeral, ran straight up the stairs to her room and threw herself down on the bed. Curled up into a ball, she rocked back and forth, holding her knees.

No more dreams, she swore to herself. I don't want to see anything ever again.

She pulled a picture off the wall next to her bed, gazing at her best friend's smiling face. She couldn't imagine what would happen if Michaela ever found out that she had known what would happen to her mother. Losing her best friend was not a risk she was willing to take, if she could help it.

And so she tried. Every night before she went to sleep, she would clear her mind. If she had a dream, she would try to forget it the minute she woke up, drowning the images in everyday things and pushing them into the farthest corners of her mind. Every day she would remember less and less. She was winning the battle.

Sometimes she would be concentrating so hard on chasing the images away, with her eyes scrunched closed and her hands balled up in fists at her sides, that she wouldn't notice the odd things that were happening around her.

It started slowly at first—it was hardly noticeable. Paivi was so focused on getting rid of the dreams that she didn't notice a small horse figurine inch slightly across the top of her dresser. She didn't see the book sliding ever so gently towards the edge of the bookshelf, where it stopped just before falling.

One day, however, as she was concentrating ever so hard on pushing a particularly happy vision from her mind, she couldn't help but notice.

Maybe it wasn't so bad to have visions, she thought to herself as she lay in her bed, staring at the ceiling after a particularly entertaining vision that occurred while she slept.

Sometimes her visions were good, really good. She closed her eyes, trying to remember the face of the boy she was kissing in her dream.

Paivi then thought back to Mrs. Brown's funeral. Trees with budding leaves framed the scene in the cemetery, softening the harsh gray of the gravestones. Bright sunlight reflected off of the pearly casket as it sat over the large hole dug in the fresh earth. The scene was almost beautiful, if it wasn't for the tragedy that lay beneath the mountain of blood-red roses that dripped red rivulets across the white lid.

Paivi felt a surge of anger push through all of her anguish. Her brain was on fire and the heat coursed through her, pulsing through her veins from her fingers to her toes. She clenched her fists and squeezed her eyes shut. She cried out in pain, unable to keep the rush of energy inside her body. It burst out through her fingertips, whipping around her. The sound of a loud crash brought her back into the room. She opened her eyes to see books flying across the room from the shelves and slamming into the wall opposite. They fell to the floor in a heap, open with pages and covers bent. Figurines of horses and unicorns as well as dolls were flying from the top of her dresser and smashing into the walls. Shards of porcelain rained down on the floor.

She stood up, looking around in amazement. It looked like a bomb had gone off. Posters had fallen to the floor and others clung to the wall in tatters. A flying hairbrush had shattered a mirror and the walls were chipped and dented from the force of the collisions. Her parents thundered up the stairs and threw open the door. Mr. and Mrs. Anderson stood in the doorway, stunned, their jaws dropped, chins almost touching their chests. They looked at each other with wide eyes and then at Paivi, bewildered by the destruction that surrounded their little girl and stunned that she stood in the middle of the chaos and was completely unscathed.

Chapter Two

Birthday Surprise

Paivi couldn't have been more excited. Friday, the fifteenth of August, was a special day. It was not just her fourteenth birthday. She was also finally getting her braces off. In all honesty, she was more excited about getting the metal contraption removed than she was about the birthday. As far as she was concerned, birthdays come around every year, but it's not every day that you get a new face.

She considered briefly that her new gleaming smile would attract a few boys, maybe a boyfriend? Okay, she didn't want to get too carried away. There were more obstacles to getting a boyfriend that a mouthful of beautiful teeth couldn't solve. At six feet tall, Paivi hoped there were more tall boys at St. Andrew High School than there had been at Riverview Junior High, otherwise she would be out of luck.

The morning of the fifteenth dawned bright and cool, as if recognizing the setting of Sirius, the Dog Star, signifying the end of the Dog Days of summer. Paivi woke to the light tinkle of wind chimes that hung from the porch below her bedroom window. The sun filtered through the purple curtains that fluttered in the light breeze. The smell of fresh waffles wafted up from the kitchen. She wasted no time getting down to breakfast.

"Happy birthday, my love!" said her mom as Paivi entered the sunny kitchen. There was a large stack of steaming golden waffles covered with powdered sugar sitting in the middle of the table. "Don't bother looking at the newspaper this morning," she added hurriedly.

"Why? Did that terrorist group blow someone else up? What else is new?" Paivi added flippantly, grabbing the front page and reading the headline '7 Dead in McDonald's Playground Attack: Righteous Front claims responsibility.'

"Righteous Front." she snorted. "I hope that makes them feel better about what they do. I mean, seriously, what's righteous about killing innocent people?"

Mrs. Anderson sighed at her daughter's nonchalant response. Attacks by the domestic terrorist group Righteous Front were so commonplace that everyone under the age of twenty thought weekly terrorist attacks were a normal fact of life.

"I just don't know what's going on anymore. I wish the government could get a handle on the situation. Hopefully one of these presidential candidates can get it right, although that Senator Stevens seems to have no new ideas. Maybe Moira Kelly. She seems to have her head on right. Those Righteous Front members are just a bunch of right-wing loonies. I know the economy is bad, but wanting to get rid of immigrants, legal or not, isn't going to solve the problem. It's not their fault! And the RF keep killing citizens too, so what are they really trying to prove? I suppose we should just be glad we haven't had any attacks by those monsters here in St. Andrew," nodded Mrs. Anderson.

"Yet," added Paivi cautiously. "Don't say that too loud, they might hear you!"

"Well, anyways, I think we are all set for today." Mrs. Anderson handed Paivi a plate and a fork and knife, happy to change the subject. "We have to be at Dr. Summers by noon. It'll probably take some time there, maybe an hour or two. And then the girls are coming over for pizza at five thirty. The movie is at eight over at the Cineplex and I think that just about covers it! So what are you excited most about today?"

"I have to say—getting my braces off! I couldn't ask for a better birthday present!"

"Well, great, that solves the problem of having to buy you a present!" said Mrs. Anderson brightly. "Now finish your birthday waffles while I go drag your brother out of bed. I swear, if I didn't get him up, he'd sleep the whole day away!"

Five thirty arrived quickly. Paivi paced back and forth in the living room, watching anxiously out the front windows, awaiting the arrival of her friends. She kept running her tongue across her smooth teeth, flashing them on and off at the mirror as she practiced different smiles. She couldn't stop looking at them.

As she glanced out the front window for the tenth time, looking for any sign of an approaching car, she heard a noise behind her and jumped.

INTO THE SHADOWS

"Jeez! You scared me!" she said as she wheeled around, clutching her hand to her heart."Gotcha!" Her younger brother Torsten hopped down the last few steps. His curly, dark hair was neatly combed and he was wearing khaki shorts and a button-down shirt. This was quite dressy compared to his normal wardrobe, which generally consisted of basketball shorts and T-shirts.

"Wait a minute, why are you so dressed up anyways? Got a hot date or something?"

"What, this?" he asked, fidgeting with his shirt collar. "I dress like this all the time. So, uh, what are you guys doing tonight? Is Aimee coming over?"

"Oh, I see! Yeah, Aimee's coming over. Only don't get your hopes up. Aimee will NOT go out with an eighth grader!" snorted Paivi.

Torsten and Paivi were complete opposites, aside from height. Paivi, with her blond hair, green eyes and fair skin was a stark contrast to her brother, with his dark brown hair, matching eyes and olive skin.

"Anyways, you know what we're doing tonight. Mom said you were supposed to leave us alone." She felt sorry as soon as she said it, it sounded so mean. "But if you want to go to the movie, I guess that would be alright."

"Yeah, but what are you going to see?" he asked, trying to sound nonchalant, even thought he was clearly excited at the prospect of spending time with Aimee.

"Well, I want to see 'Sweet Pete', that new romantic comedy," she said.

"Seriously? That's what you want to go see? God,

anything is better than that! I would rather get punched in the stomach than see that movie"

"It's MY birthday. No one said you had to go!" she sputtered.

"It's going to be terrible, I hope you know that," he said condescendingly.

"Look, we are GIRLS. We like romantic comedies. If you ever want to get a girlfriend, you better get used to it, quick!" she shouted at him. As she stormed upstairs to her room, she heard a picture frame crash to the floor behind her. She cringed, but didn't turn around.

"God, you walk like such an elephant! The picture just fell off the wall! I'm telling Mom!"

She'd rather her mom think her heavy feet had caused the picture to fall, but Paivi knew it had nothing to do her stomping. After demolishing her room so many years ago, she had tried very hard to control her anger. Many times she could feel the energy well up in her, and with a few deep breaths it would subside. She didn't want her friends or anyone at school to know her secret. What would they say? She didn't want to be seen as a grade-A freak. The whole seeing-the-future-thing was much easier to hide, though it ate at her every time she thought of Michaela.

"Oooooo! Your teeth look AWESOME, Paivi!" Michaela squealed as she dragged their friends Aimee Watson and Crystal Harris through the front door.

"Definitely hot," agreed Jenn Hernandez as she and Paulina Kaminski followed the group inside.

INTO THE SHADOWS

"Thanks! Come on in, I think my dad just got back with the pizzas," she said, waving them towards the kitchen.

After a few thick slices of Chicago-style pizza and an impromptu burping contest, Mrs. Anderson brought out a thick and fudgy chocolate cake. They sang 'Happy Birthday' to Paivi very loudly and off key.

"Make a wish!" shouted Paulina.

A wish. Paivi stopped and looked at the candles.

Normal, she thought. I wish for a nice, normal freshman year. Oh, and maybe a boyfriend. Yeah, that would be nice!

She closed her eyes and blew on the candles, the tiny flames flickering and then going out.

Brightly wrapped birthday presents were then passed to Paivi, which she happily tore open. Picture frame, silver necklace, photo album, clothes and CDs; overall it wasn't a bad haul.

The last gift was in a small and wrapped in bright pink paper with a silver bow. She picked up the box and shook it, trying to hear what was inside, but it made no noise. She tore off the wrapping to reveal a delicate mahogany box. The wood looked old but was still shiny and dark. The lid displayed an expertly carved design. There were some words in a strange language engraved in a circle around the edges and a metal closure on the front. Paivi pressed what looked to be a tiny button and the clasp popped open. She lifted the lid, revealing the most beautiful locket she had ever seen.

It was small and round, a little larger than a quarter.

Around the edges it was finely polished silver, which surrounded a circle of gold. In the center was a Celtic knot shaped like a triangle, inlaid in silver. She turned the locket over, and saw some more unfamiliar writing engraved around the edge. The chain that hung from the locket was of thick silver and looked heavy, but it was surprisingly light. It resembled a metal chain, only in miniature. She ran the chain through her fingers, turning the locket over and over in her hands. She pulled it open to find it empty on one half. The other half contained a mirror.

"Wow Mom," said Paivi. "Where did you get this?"

"The locket has been in our family for generations," she started, "and now I am passing it on to you."

"How cool," said Michaela. "Ooo, pass it around, I want to see it!"

"Sure, here." Paivi passed the locket to Jenn, who paused to give it a look before passing it around the table.

"Mrs. A.," started Paulina, as she turned the locket over in her hands, "what does the writing say here? What language is this anyways?"

"It's Gaelic. My relatives back in Ireland used to speak it, but sadly it's not something they passed on to us after moving to America. Unfortunately I'm not quite sure what it says."

"That's too bad," said Paulina. "Well, whatever it says, it's really pretty!"

"Thanks, everyone, for the best birthday ever!" Paivi glanced at the clock on the wall. "Oh! It's getting late! We've gotta go if we're going to make the movie!"

"I am so tired." Paivi walked through the kitchen after they returned from dropping off her friends, basking in the pink and purple streamers, balloons, and presents strewn across the table.

I love my birthday! she thought to herself with a sigh. I wish I could have more than one a year!

"Paivi," started her mother, pulling her out of her birthday bliss. "And Torsten," she continued. "Don't go upstairs just yet, your father and I would like to have a word with you both."

"Did we do something wrong?" Paivi asked, trying to think if she had done anything punishable in the recent past. She glanced at Torsten, his brain clearly hard at work.

"Do either of you want a piece of cake?" Mr. Anderson cut a huge piece for himself and dumped it on a plate.

"Oooo yes please!" answered Paivi. Cake was always good.

Torsten took a piece as well and they carried their plates to the family room, where they settled into the couches.

The family room was large, with two tall windows flanking the stone fireplace. Along the wooden mantel was a collection of family photos, showing Paivi and Torsten posing in uniform with a basketball alongside pictures of them as chubby little babies. The room was filled with overstuffed leather furniture that looked like it belonged in an English pub.

Mr. and Mrs. Anderson sank into the couch across from Paivi and Torsten. Paivi looked at her parents and could see something on their faces, but she couldn't quite figure out what it was. She glanced at Torsten to see if he had noticed anything, but he only had eyes for his cake. He was shoveling large chunks of it into his mouth so quickly that he didn't notice the large smear of frosting on his cheek.

"We have something to tell you, and we know you will have a lot of questions," began Mrs. Anderson.

"Are you getting a divorce?" asked Torsten, wiping the frosting off his cheek with the back of his hand, which he then licked clean. Between licks, he continued. "Because if I have to pick someone to live with—well I just can't do it. I'll have to split it evenly because I like you both equally," he hesitated for a second, "okay, well maybe I would pick Mom. Sorry Dad, but she's much cleaner."

"No Tor, we are not getting a divorce. But it's nice to know who's side you're on, just in case!" laughed Mr. Anderson.

It seemed to lighten the mood a little bit, and when Mrs. Anderson began again, she sounded less nervous.

"Okay, well you both are aware that Paivi has sometimes had dreams where she can see things that later happen," she paused.

"Oh yeah!" interrupted Torsten. "Like the time she had that dream that I was going to fall off the slide at the park and break my arm and then I did! That was crazy!"

"Not only that, we later learned that Paivi can move things without touching them. However, that has only

INTO THE SHADOWS

happened once, as far as we know. You remember that night a few years ago when your room was, well... a bit destroyed?" she asked, looking at Paivi.

Paivi looked a bit sheepish.

"It does still happen sometimes," she said quietly.

"Why didn't you tell us honey?" asked Mrs. Anderson, sounding concerned.

"That's why, that tone in your voice. I didn't want to worry you." She played with her piece of cake, not quite able to take another bite. "You were so worried and upset when I trashed my room, I just didn't want to make it worse. And besides, it was just little things that moved around, not like the time you're talking about."

"Wait a minute!" sputtered Torsten, sitting forward in his chair and nearly dropping his plate and fork onto the dark hardwood floor. "Let me get this straight. That time when your room was destroyed and everything was smashed to bits, you, YOU did that?"

"Yes Tor, you have to understand, you were so young, we couldn't just tell you the truth. We had trouble with it, and we were grownups!" responded Mrs. Anderson.

"You told me it was a crazed squirrel that came in through the window!" he said sulkily, setting down his plate and folding his arms as he sank back into the couch, pouting.

"That's right," Mr. Anderson chuckled. "I forgot about the crazed squirrel!"

"I was always afraid he'd come back and attack me in my sleep!" Torsten softened a little, letting out a giggle.

The memory even brought a laugh out of Paivi and

her mother.

"Okay, so here's my first question," said Paivi. "Can Tor do anything," she paused, turning towards him. "Do you have dreams or can you move stuff?"

"Not that I know of! I wish!" said Torsten. "Why can't I do the same things as Paivi, Mom and Dad?"

"You might someday," began Mr. Anderson. "Our families have a long history of these special abilities. Both of our families have what are called Seers. A Seer is someone who receives visions of the future. As far as we know, they can't be controlled. Your mother and I see things in our dreams also. As for you, Tor, some people take a little longer to discover their abilities. But it is also possible that you will never develop any."

"Nice. Figures, Paivi gets all of the cool stuff," whined Torsten.

"Look, it's not like I wanted this stuff. Some of the things I've seen," she paused, seeing the image of Mrs. Brown and the burning car, "I wish I never had—they were awful."

Paivi shivered, a chill spilling down her spine. She set down what was left of her cake and pulled her knees in, wrapping her arms around them.

"So what," said Torsten, irritated. "Then you can just do something about it if you don't like what you see."

"No," said Mr. Anderson. "As a Seer, you have to follow one rule – you cannot interfere with what you see."

"Well, that's stupid!" said Torsten. "What's the point of being able to see the future if you can't do anything about it?"

"This rule goes back to ancient times," replied Mrs. Anderson. "This is what my mother told me. Let's say in Mrs. Brown's case that you had told her to stay home that day. The event may have still occurred, but then it could affect someone else's life in turn. Someone may have taken Mrs. Brown's place that day, maybe a young girl riding with her parents or someone's grandfather. It is not for us to choose who lives and dies. That is way too much responsibility for one person to have. Besides, if you did get involved, you would begin to obsess over your visions, frantically trying to save everyone you know. Everyone's story has a different ending and unfortunately we aren't the writers, just the readers. There are some visions that can change. The event may not occur because the people involved alter the outcome of the situation— they make different choices. It's not that the vision you had was wrong; it could be that it was just one option. If we were to get involved, we could disrupt it somehow, upset the balance."

"So, Dad, if you can do this too, do you use it to catch bad guys while you are at work?" asked Paivi.

"It may help to know who I'm looking for, but we still have to have evidence. I can't just run around rounding up criminals with no case against them. People would get suspicious. They would wonder where I had gotten my information," Mr. Anderson said.

"Why would anyone care?" asked Paivi. "You're just trying to help people."

"That comes to the most important part of the

discussion. People who don't have this ability wouldn't understand that we are special and not just a bunch of freaks. For centuries our ancestors had to carry the knowledge of these gifts in complete secrecy. Before the Middle Ages, people with special abilities were respected and trusted," said Mr. Anderson. "There were magicians, sorcerers or viziers on every royal court. You know, Grandpa Anderson did a family tree a few years back and found that we had some very interesting relatives. He claims that Merlin Ambrosius, the Sorcerer of King Arthur's court, was a second cousin, twice removed. He also discovered relatives who lost their lives during the Spanish Inquisition and even a great-great-great aunt that died in the Salem Witch Trials here in the U.S. If they didn't agree that they were receiving visions from God, they were put to death as witches. Those with special abilities who believed God spoke through them became powerful within the church. Many of them are saints we know today."

"Huh, so saints were really just people like me. Interesting," Paivi said. "But how awful for the others; why didn't these people get together and do something about it?"

"Well, we aren't superheroes honey!" chuckled Mrs. Anderson. "And there are not huge numbers of people like us. They were split up pretty far and wide back then, it was nearly impossible for them to contact each other. They were forced to keep their secrets in order to survive. Some families moved near others they knew, but that was dangerous as well. It was difficult to trust anyone. Now times are different. We might still keep a distance from others, but they make themselves known to us, and us to them."

"Wait!" shouted Torsten. "There are more people like this in St. Andrew? Who are they? Do we know them?"

"That is our secret to keep," said Mrs. Anderson. "We can't allow information like that to be passed to children. It's our choice to tell you about all of this, but it's not fair for us to put others into jeopardy by naming names."

"Well, how do you know who they are then? I thought you all tried to keep separated from each other," asked Paivi.

"There is a way to tell about the others, a sign, but you can only see it if you know what you are looking for. When you are eighteen and an adult, we will explain it to you. But until then, mum's the word," said Mrs. Anderson.

"And the others, can we all do the same things?" Paivi had a million questions running through her mind.

"Some, but it's possible that there are abilities out there that we have never seen or heard of yet. Being that we have to keep it all to ourselves, we can never be sure what others are capable of, or for that matter, what they are doing with it," answered Mr. Anderson, laying his empty cake plate on the wooden coffee table.

"We chose to make use of our abilities only for good things, but others may not make the same choices. These things can be dangerous. For instance, those 'Illusionists' that perform in Las Vegas and make those television shows doing their street magic are putting us all in jeopardy. They think they have everyone convinced that it's just entertainment. All so they can make a quick buck and hang out with their Hollywood friends. It's such a great risk to us all," said Mrs. Anderson with a hint of disapproval.

Paivi thought of the locket in its velvet-lined box. She had an urge to put it on. "And the locket? I know everyone was here earlier, so you couldn't really say much, but do you know any more about it, really?"

"No, my mother told me when she gave it to me that if I ever needed something, it would be there for me. But in thirty years, I've never noticed it do anything. I think she was just trying to give me a romantic story to make the locket more special. Anyways, it's pretty." The carved wooden clock on the mantel chimed once. "Oh, I didn't realize how late it was getting!"

Mrs. Anderson jumped up from the couch, grabbing her plate and an empty glass from the coffee table. She put her things in the kitchen and turned back to her children, giving them both a big hug as they rose from the couch. "Now don't forget to put your dishes in the dishwasher! Let's get to bed!"

It took Paivi a long time to fall asleep that night. Her mind felt full, and trying to close her eyes felt like trying to shut the doors on an over-stuffed garage. She pulled back the curtain, staring out the window at the full moon floating in the starry sky. The moonlight turned the street in front of the house into a river of silver. She begged sleep to come, and as dawn brightened on the horizon, with Mr. Teddy Bear in her arms, Paivi finally drifted off to sleep.

Chapter Three
Back to School

Paivi was up before her alarm, both nervous and excited about the first day of high school. She got ready quickly and made her way down to grab a bowl of cereal before heading out to the bus stop. She stepped around bags and people in the aisle, finally finding a seat near the middle of the bus. Being the first day back, no one had found older kids to ride to school with just yet. There was no air conditioning on the bus, just a hot, humid rush of air through all of the open windows, which caused Paivi to rethink her wardrobe choice. Her new jeans were sticking to her legs. She just kept reminding herself that the school would be like a meat locker, so it would pay off in the end.

  The bus joined the queue in the driveway in front of the school, pulling slowly forward, and opened the doors to allow their passengers to exit. Paivi took the steps slowly. It would be extremely embarrassing to fall down the stairs in front of the whole school. Not quite the impression she was going for. She stepped off the bus into a throng of students and was shuffled towards the courtyard, where everyone split off into their own groups. Some students continued on, filtering through the front doors and into the cafeteria.

Paivi decided to stay outside to see if she could find Michaela or any of the other girls. They had all come on different buses. She waved and greeted a few kids she remembered from junior high, but kept walking. She found a spot along the concrete wall and sat for a minute, taking in her surroundings.

St. Andrew High School was a very uninteresting looking building. The original school had been built in 1872 and was an imposing building of brick and stone that resembled a castle. As St. Andrew grew, the building became too small, and the new St. Andrew High School was built down the street. It opened in 1971, apparently when no one had any sort of creativity regarding architecture and design. The school was large and boxy, like someone had just gone and glued some rectangles together. The building was covered in red brick and the only good thing about it was the fact that it had large windows that looked out onto a forest preserve.

"Hey P!" Paivi heard a familiar voice behind her. She spun around and saw Michaela and Paulina walking towards her.

"Can you believe it's our first day!" squealed Michaela rubbing her hands together. "Just think of all the new boys. And OLDER boys! Nice!"

The three of them turned to see a large group of boys looking in their direction. When they noticed they had been caught, they quickly looked away, shouting at each other and laughing. There was one boy that caught Paivi's eye. He looked right at her, unblinking. His cold stare made her slightly uncomfortable. He held her gaze a moment longer and then broke it, turning back to his friends.

"Oooo!" said Michaela, teasing Paivi as she nudged her in the ribs with her elbow. "It looks like somebody's got a thing for you, P! Nice job! The first bell hasn't even rung yet!"

Paivi let out a nervous laugh as the bell rang and the throng of students moved in a giant wave, carrying them all towards the door.

The day was a mixture of feelings. It was exciting to see old friends after months apart, which resulted in large groups of screaming and hugging girls. There was also tension as they checked out the new students, possible friends and enemies that they hadn't met yet. They attempted to size each other up without appearing obvious. The classes themselves were the dullest part of the day, more so for the fact that every teacher spent the period 'getting to know' their new students by playing cheesy ice-breaker games and going over never-ending lists of classroom rules. In each class they collected book after book until they were teetering precariously through the hallways, hoping to make it to their lockers before their backs gave out.

Paivi stumbled into her sixth period class balancing a pile of books and notebooks and collapsed into the nearest open seat. The desk was old and not quite level, and when she dropped her pile onto it, everything proceeded to slide onto the floor with a loud crash.

She looked at the heap of books and paper, put her

hand to her head and sighed loudly. She bent down, stacking the items one by one on the desk.

"Looks like you might want to invest in a backpack, unless you happen to turn into the Incredible Hulk during passing periods," said an unfamiliar voice dryly, as a hand reached down from the desk across the aisle and began picking up a few of her books.

"Uh, yeah, thanks. I left it in my locker. I just didn't think we would get so much stuff already!" She slammed the last book onto the pile, and finally looked up. The owner of the voice across the aisle handed Paivi her things stacked neatly, which she set next to her sloppy pile, hoping to avoid a repeat performance.

"Thanks for your help," Paivi said, smiling at him.

"No problem! Just try to keep those books under control!" He held out his hand. "I'm Jason, by the way."

She took Jason's hand and shook it strongly. His brown eyes sparkled in the fluorescent lights and she noticed how his dark hair complimented his smooth, cocoa skin.

"I'm Paivi." She felt her heart flutter in her chest and hoped her face wasn't turning a bright shade of pink.

"Paivi? Well that's one I haven't heard before. What does it mean?" He turned sideways in the desk to look at her.

"It means 'day' in Finnish," she explained. "We still have some cousins that are like eight times removed that live there."

"Finland? I heard Santa Claus lives there! Nice!" He laughed.

She groaned. "Yeah, it's great."

"So, why did you take this class?" he asked as he stuck a pencil behind his ear.

"Last spring when we were picking classes, I decided that I wanted to take Intro to Law, but when I went to my guidance counselor, the girl in front of me beat me to it and took the last seat. This class was open, and it sounded kind of interesting."

At that moment, Paivi's friend Crystal bounded through the classroom door and plopped herself into the seat behind Paivi.

"Hey, P, do you think they'll let us keep these seats?" she asked, pulling out a tube of lip gloss.

"I doubt it— most teachers make you sit alphabetically. Oh, Crystal, this is Jason."

The introduction was cut short as an explosion of bright fabrics, wild hair, and papers flew through the door.

"Hello, everyone, hello!" an older woman shouted, sounding a bit flustered as she dropped the pile of books and papers onto the desk at the front of the room. The woman took a deep breath and looked around the room as she attempted to straighten her hair and her blouse at the same time with very little success. Little wisps of blond permed hair continued to float around her head, making her look like she had been struck by lightning. It almost seemed like her hair was frantically trying to escape. Her navy and red suit was a bit disheveled and her shoes were black. Paivi wondered if the woman had bothered to look in the mirror before she left this morning.

It took her a few moments before she realized she

had failed to introduce herself.

"Oh! My name is Dr. Hasenpfeffer. Welcome to Current Events."

The students said nothing.

"There is no text for this class," the students perked up a bit, "I will supply all of the necessary materials. In this class we will look at our current world and domestic problems such as terrorism and poverty. We will learn about the media and also about other countries that affect us daily, though you may not realize it."

The students were all waiting anxiously for Dr. Hasenpfeffer to move them into new seats. She said nothing about it and they were afraid to mention it. No one wanted to be responsible for giving her the idea. She spent the rest of the period discussing the outsourcing of jobs, terrorist attacks in the United States since 2001, and her cat, Clarence. Apparently he was suffering from a chronic hairball condition.

The bell rang, and the students jumped up, quickly making their way out of the classroom. Crystal was shaking her head as they exited.

"Honestly, we aren't supposed to remember any of that stuff, are we?" Crystal moaned.

"Well, I hope how many hairballs Clarence tosses in a normal week and how that effects global warming is not on the final," quipped Jason, as they all laughed.

"I feel like my brain was just pulled in ten directions! I can't possibly understand what she is a doctor of! Thank God it's time for lunch. Anybody else have lunch this hour?" Paivi patted her stomach.

"Not me! Later!" Crystal waved as she made her way in the opposite direction.

Paivi and Jason wound their way through the crowded hallways down to the cafeteria, both being unfortunate enough to have the very last lunch hour of the day. But at least they could finally relax; it was nearly the end of the first day of classes.

"So, are you meeting any friends in lunch?" asked Jason.

"Yeah, luckily my best friend, Michaela, has it too. What about you?"

"I've got some friends in here too. Although I don't know how easy it'll be to find them." He looked around the mayhem in the cafeteria. Hundreds of students wandered around aimlessly, looking for their friends. The smart ones headed straight for the lunch lines, deciding food was more important. Paivi saw Michaela out of the corner of her eye. She was standing on her seat in the far corner of the cafeteria, waving her arms wildly in the air in order to get Paivi's attention. A lunch monitor ran up and began scolding her to get down.

Paivi laughed and pointed to Michaela. "I am sad to say I found my friend. I better get over there before she gets herself thrown out! See you tomorrow!"

"Later!" Jason headed off in the other direction.

Paivi made her way through the maze of tables where Michaela and Aimee had saved her a seat. Michaela was promising the lunch monitor that she would never misuse school property again in such a fashion. She sat back down out of breath.

"Getting in trouble already? It's only the first day!" laughed Paivi.

"Just be glad you didn't have to wander around like some idiot to find us in this mess!" She sounded mad, but Paivi knew better. Michaela suddenly brightened. "And who, may I ask, was the cute guy you were with?"

"I wasn't WITH a guy—he's just some guy from my Current Events class."

"What's his deal? Does he have a girlfriend or what? What grade is he in?" Michaela demanded.

"I just met him today. I'm sorry I didn't manage to get his life story. But I'll keep you posted. Better yet, I can introduce you and you can interrogate him yourself," Paivi giggled. She scanned the room, looking to see where Jason was sitting. She hoped the others didn't notice. No luck. She leaned back in her seat, contemplating whether she should attempt the lunch line, when she saw him. Unfortunately it was not Jason—instead it was the boy she had seen earlier that morning. And he was sitting just four tables away. She couldn't help but look. He wasn't so creepy when he wasn't staring her down. He must have felt her eyes, however, and turned his head slowly, his eyes meeting hers. They were as cold and icy as before and she could feel the hair on the back of her neck stand up. She pulled her eyes away quickly, looking towards Michaela, hoping he would look away too. But he did not.

This is ridiculous! she thought to herself. How can I

be afraid of someone I don't even know? This is stupid.

She stood up, still avoiding his gaze. "Are you guys ready to get some food?"

The three girls headed to the front of the cafeteria and joined the line.

Chapter Four
Open Seas

Paivi Anderson
Current Events p.6
Dr. Hasenpfeffer

For my assignment I read an article in the <u>St. Andrew Herald</u> by Jerome Knowles. It was called "Moira Kelly takes the lead in the polls." He states that Kelly, a member of the Liberal party, is ahead in the polls because Americans think she's personable. That means she nice. He also says that her policies on the Righteous Front terrorist group are helping her. She hopes to solve the terrorist crisis by sitting down and talking to the members of the Righteous Front. The current administration has been fighting the RF with the military, but the RF keeps blowing up more restaurants and shopping malls. According to Knowles, Senator Stevens represents the same ideas as the current President who is also from the Conservative party and will not have much of a chance with the voters. I personally think it's because he's not very nice, but that's just because he looks like a jerk when I see him on the news.

Into the Shadows

Paivi, interesting opinions, but try to keep them relevant to the facts. B-

Dr. H.

The full moon shone over the water creating a silver path on the waves that disappeared into the horizon, a road straight to the heavens. A yacht cut directly across the light and then in a moment, it was gone, returning to the shadows.

An older man sat in a leather chair next to the window looking out over the waves. In the distance he could see the city of Miami glittering like so many giant candles floating on the water. His gray hair had become a bit wavy due to the humidity. He had long ago given up on his tie and jacket: now his collar was unbuttoned, and the shirtsleeves on his hand-tailored dress shirt were rolled up to the elbows. The crisp white cotton had wilted in the steamy heat and large rings of sweat seeped from underneath his heavy arms. In his hand he nervously clinked the dwindling ice in his glass, pausing only to refill it from the decanter of bourbon sitting on the small table next to him.

Taking a swig of his drink, he jumped—startled—as the door at the end of the room popped open. A young man peered cautiously into the room.

"Senator Stevens, we are nearly there," said the young man.

"Thank you Martin." He spoke with a southern drawl. The Senator finished his drink and took one last look at the water.

The deckhands took no time in connecting the

Senator's yacht to a new, larger and more brilliantly lit one. The man and his party—consisting of Martin and a young woman by the name of Margaret— made their way across a metal bridge. Upon stepping onto the glossy wooden deck, they were met by two men. The one who greeted them was rather small. His companion, however, was quite an intimidating figure of substantial size, not to mention the two large handguns he wore in holsters strapped across his broad chest.

"Ahhh, Senator Stevens, how nice to see you again." He smiled, revealing a toothy grin.

"Follow us, please." He led the man and his companions along the glistening deck to the back of the yacht, where they climbed a staircase towards the ship's rooftop. Each stair was lit with tiny, twinkling lights.

As the first sight of the uppermost level came into view, torches danced along the railings, throwing brilliant light and dark shadows across the deck. A few young ladies in sparkling evening gowns lounged along the banks of seats under the torches. They leaned back, sipping champagne and chatting quietly.

At the far end of the deck a man rose from a lounge chair. He was fairly tall and wore a pair of white linen pants and a loose-fitting white linen shirt. He was barefoot.

"Your friends can wait here—the girls will bring you a drink." Their escort stopped them at the top of the stairs and waved Senator Stevens on alone. He walked across the deck, trying not to notice the men with machine guns standing on either side of his host.

36

"Senator Stevens," greeted the man, sounding relaxed. He shook his guest's hand briefly. "Please, sit. Here, have some champagne, you look like you could use it."

Senator Stevens accepted the delicate crystal champagne flute, but just held it, as if not quite sure what he should to do with it.

"Mr. Lin, it's truly my pleasure," began the Senator, sounding as if it wasn't a pleasure at all. "I take it you have the information you promised?"

"Ahh, right to the point, aren't you? I thought we could at least share a drink first. But here is what you came for." He gracefully placed a small, USB flash drive into Senator Stevens' plump and sweaty hand.

"This is it? This will help me win?" He stared at the little drive in disbelief.

"Please let us recall, you requested some information, something that no one else has, that could help you win your precious election. The information you seek is on that drive."

"So what is it? Dirty photos? Information exposing bribes? What?"

"No. What you have in your hands is a list of names. These names will be worth more than all the money in your campaign fund."

"Names? So what? Names alone won't do me any good," Senator Stevens was getting angry, and losing his already strained ability to be polite.

Lin smiled calmly and leaned forward.

"Your country lives in fear because of your constant

37

battles with the terrorists. What do they call themselves? The Righteous Front? Ha! But all along you have had the answer to stopping them—you just didn't know about it. You see, these are names of people who live in your country. You will be surprised to find that they know more about these Righteous Front fellows than you could ever imagine. Your staff should be able to come up with a plan that will benefit you greatly." He leaned back on his lounge chair and sipped his champagne, smiling at the elegance of his own actions.

"You must be crazy. Do you think I am going to pay you millions for a list of names? This meeting is over!" Senator Stevens rose clumsily from his chair, holding the flash drive out to him.

"Senator, I guarantee you that I am perfectly sane. And yes, you will pay." Lin snapped his fingers and one of his large guards jumped forward, coming to his boss' side. He mumbled some instructions in Chinese and the guard was released, striding over to the small group and snatching a surprised Martin by the shoulder. He half-dragged Martin across the deck, presenting him to his master.

"The receipt, young man?" Lin held out his hand expectantly.

Martin hurriedly produced an envelope from his pocket, handing it over to Lin's perfectly manicured hands.

"It's been a pleasure doing business with you, Senator Stevens," he said, raising himself slowly out of his chair. "Chen will show you out."

The man stepped forward, gesturing for the group to follow him. Chen lead them back to the side of the large yacht, where they clambered, one by one, back onto the less impressive vessel.

Senator Stevens' yacht departed and moved quietly through the now-dark water, making its way back to the glittering lights of Miami.

The Senator resumed his position in the leather chair next to the window and was absentmindedly clinking the ice in his glass once again. Noticing the glass was empty; he reached for the decanter, but realized that it too, was empty.

"Martin." He was waving the decanter in the air. "Go get this filled up for me. And Maggie, sugar, why don't you load up this drive and see what we've got."

"Yes sir!" they both answered simultaneously, rushing to appease him.

Martin hurriedly left the room while Margaret pulled a chair and table next to the Senator. She set a sleek laptop on the table and opened it, settling herself into the chair. She plugged the small drive into the laptop and began to open the files.

"Well, sir, it looks like the lists are broken down by state. Oh, and here, also Washington, D.C.," she said, pointing out the list of folders on the screen. "What exactly are we looking for then?"

"I am very much hoping you will be able to help me figure that out, Miss Maggie," he drawled, patting her hand. Maggie smiled uncomfortably. "Well, go ahead and open that Washington, D.C. file. We know a lot of people there. Maybe it'll give us a clue."

Margaret clicked on the folder and up popped a

document.
The first name on the list read:
Ackemann, Martin
102 W. 9th Street
Washington, D.C., 20013
Married: No Age: 29
Employer: Assistant to U.S. Senator Wendell Stevens
Ability: Mind Reader

"What does this mean, sir?" Margaret's brows furrowed in confusion.

Senator Stevens said nothing, his jaw dropped slightly in a stunned silence. At that moment, the door opened and Martin came into the room, carrying the newly filled decanter and a tray topped with freshly baked chocolate chip cookies.

"Felipe just finished these. He thought we could use some chocolate." He set the decanter and the tray of cookies gently down on the table, failing to notice the other two staring at him intently, eyes wide. He looked up and jumped back a little.

"What's going on?" he asked cautiously, his hand nervously toying with his loosened necktie. "Why are you staring at me like that?"

"Because, Martin, you're the first name on this list that I just received from my associate. He said the people on this list might know something about the Righteous Front that could help us. Judging by the ability listed here on this sheet — Mind Reader — it appears you know way more about a lot of things than we could have ever expected. But first we need to know whose side you're on. Well, Martin?" They continued to stare at him, now sitting slightly forward in their chairs peering through the thick tension in the air.

Martin instantly paled, looking as if he might be sick.

"Sir, I...uh...I can explain," he stuttered.

"I certainly hope so." The Senator smiled smugly, relaxing back into his chair, but not before grabbing a cookie from the tray and taking a big bite.

Chapter Five

Homecoming

The gym was decorated with Christmas trees and large, wrapped presents. Snowflakes hung from the ceiling along with clear twinkle lights. There was a dusting of fake snow on the ground. A large reindeer with a glowing nose stood in a small grove of evergreens in a corner. A snowman, along with Santa and his sleigh were displayed in another.

Students were heading towards the dance floor. Girls were dressed in elegant floor length dresses in rich colors of velvet, some with long white gloves. The boys sported freshly pressed shirts and pants, with festive holiday ties.

Paivi looked around, taking in the scene before her. It truly was a 'Winter Wonderland,' as the banner that hung on the DJ booth stated. Someone had come up behind her and put a hand on her arm. She turned to find Jason standing there, a smile on his cheery face. She looked down to see his tie, where a line of elves were doing a Rockette-style kick line under Christmas lights, which were lit up by a small battery pack behind the tie. It was extremely cheesy, but somehow he made it look cool.

"Would you like to dance?" he asked, looking out at the dance floor as the DJ put on a slow song.

"Sure."

He put his arms around her waist and pulled her close. She put hers around his neck and rested her head on his shoulder. As happy as she should have been, she suddenly felt extremely sad. Her eyes prickled with tears and she closed them tight. A few escaped, rolling down her cheeks. She hugged him closer and whispered, "I'm sorry."

She awoke wiping her face, her cheeks wet. It had become no secret that she liked Jason, but he had a girlfriend. And the Christmas dance was still months away. She was excited to see he was her date, but why would it end in tears? It made no sense. Being with Jason was nothing to be sad about.

A lovely smell wafted underneath her bedroom door. Paivi felt her stomach growl and rolled over. The alarm clock on her nightstand read 10:12.

Ahh, she thought, I LOVE Saturdays!

She kicked off her down comforter and gave a loud yawn and a stretch, pulling herself out of bed.

Down in the kitchen she found Torsten eating a large plate of waffles doused in syrup. Mr. and Mrs. Anderson were manning the waffle iron.

"I love waffles!" she exclaimed, pulling her chair up to the kitchen table.

"Me too!" Torsten spoke through a mouthful.

"How did float building for the Homecoming Parade go last night?" inquired Mr. Anderson, trying to get a waffle off the iron without burning his fingers.

"It was great! You should see our float! The theme is 'St. Andrew goes to Hollywood.' We used chicken wire to make the Hollywood hills, that's why my hands are all scratched up." She showed her hands that were full of long red marks. "On the hills we are going to put 'SAHS' instead of 'Hollywood.' And then there is a huge shark, like Jaws, that comes out of the middle of the field and he has a Dundee Warrior in its' mouth, all covered with fake blood. On the side it says 'Chomp the Warriors.' It's really cool!"

"It sounds kind of dumb," said Torsten as he dumped half a bottle of syrup on what was left of his waffles.

"Oh shut up!" She threw a crumpled napkin across the table at him and hit him square in the head. "You're just jealous because you're still in eighth grade, you baby."

"More waffles are ready!" Mrs. Anderson brought a steaming plate to the table.

Paivi and Torsten both reached across the table, forks at the ready. Paivi gave Torsten a quick poke in the hand with her fork and then used it to spear two fluffy waffles.

"Owww! Mom! She totally stabbed me with her fork!" He pulled his hand back, rubbing it.

"Well, Tor, quit hogging all of the waffles! Serves you right!" laughed Mr. Anderson, bringing his own plate to the table. "So when is this Homecoming Dance that my little girl is going to?"

"Oooo, do you have a date? Did you find someone

tall enough to dance with?" teased Torsten.

"No, dummy, if you don't have a boyfriend, you just go with your friends. I'm going with Michaela, Crystal and Aimee. Jenn and Paulina both have boyfriends so they are going with them. But I think we all want to go to dinner together at Armando's before the dance."

"Sooo...," Torsten was trying to sound casual, "Aimee doesn't have a date then?"

"Why? Do you want to go with her? Oh wait, oh that's right, eighth graders aren't allowed!" she laughed.

"Well," interrupted her mother, "I wouldn't make too much fun of my baby boy. Next year he'll be joining you at school. Then he can go everywhere you can, so get used to it!"

Mrs. Anderson patted his head and gave him a big hug. Torsten hugged her back and stuck his tongue out at Paivi.

The week of Homecoming had Paivi feeling like she was caught in a whirlwind. Between Powder Puff, the Pep Rally, the parade, and the big game on Friday night, Paivi was lucky to at least keep up with her homework. Sleep, however, would have to wait.

Before the dance on Saturday night, Paivi and her friends gathered at Paulina's house to take group photos before heading out to dinner. Paivi towered above the group, as usual. She wore a light pink cocktail dress, which came just above her knee, along with fancy silver flip-flops instead of dress shoes. She didn't mind being taller than everyone, but she didn't want to wear heels and feel like a complete giant. Mrs. Anderson had curled her long, blond hair into ringlets and stuck in a few of her grandmother's antique hairpins.

"Here's your corsage, my lovely date," Michaela said as she pulled a box containing a flower from her purse. It was made of delicate, tiny, pink roses with sweet smelling baby's breath. Being that they didn't have dates, they agreed to buy each other corsages. Paivi had gotten Michaela's with red roses to match her long, red, sequined dress.

Michaela twirled in front of Paivi, showing off her look.

"Girl, you should be walking down the red carpet for real!" Paivi said. She admired Michaela's elaborate up-do. It pained her to think that Michaela's mother was missing her daughter's first high school dance.

Paivi grabbed Michaela's arm and led her over to the group of waiting girls. The cameras flashed as Paivi tried to keep her smile frozen to her face. She wasn't going to let anything ruin their fun tonight.

"Mmmm, my stomach is going to explode," Michaela gasped as she and Paivi made their way to the decorated entrance of the high school. She clutched her stomach with both hands. "Must…not…eat…so much pasta next time!"

"Just because it was all-you-can-eat didn't mean you had to eat it all!" Paivi giggled and followed a red carpet through the cafeteria to the doors of the gym. On either side were members of Student Council with cameras, snapping pictures of the girls as if they were famous movie stars. The school mascot, the Terrible Tartan, was waiting to escort them down the aisle. Paivi giggled at his short plaid kilt, which displayed the school colors of maroon and cream. They entered through a large archway made of fake palm trees and made their way across the floor to their friends.

Paivi saw Jason a few times in the crowd, but avoided eye contact. She wasn't sure if she was up to meeting his girlfriend. Unfortunately, she could see he'd noticed her. There was no avoiding it now.

"Hey, Paivi, I was just talking about you," Jason shouted to Paivi after he half-dragged a petite girl halfway across the floor. "This is my girlfriend, Melissa."

Paivi took the girl's limp hand in hers and shook it. Melissa produced a half smile, but said nothing.

"It's nice to meet you," Paivi said, attempting a sincere smile, even though jealousy was slowly creeping through her. She brushed it off as she waved goodbye. Her eyes followed Jason as he walked away, his arm around Melissa. Next up was a slow song, driving all of the non-couples from the dance floor.

"Let's go get something to drink," said Michaela, hooking her arm through Paivi's and pulling her off the floor. "I'm parched!"

Paivi gave the dance floor a quick glance, spotting Jason and Melissa, arms around each other, swaying to the music. Their eyes were locked on each other. She wasn't quite sure why she felt the need to look; why torture herself more?

The girls headed out to the cafeteria, where tables had been set up for refreshments.

Paivi was relieved to get a break from the hot gym. They joined a line at the table where cookies were spread out on silver trays. The group of students in front of them made their selections and finally moved on.

Paivi glanced briefly over the table and something caught her eye. She looked closer at the display. She blinked her eyes, not sure if what she saw was real. It must be a coincidence. The cookies were arranged on the table to spell out something she recognized right away.

PAIVI

Michaela was chattering on about something that Paivi didn't hear.

She noticed and put her hand on her hip.

"Hey, P, you aren't even listening to me!"

She started to pout and then noticed the strange look on Paivi's face.

"What's wrong?"

"Mick, do you notice anything about these cookies?" she asked, still staring at them.

"I don't even know what you're talking about. I think they look good and I want to eat them all."

"Yeah, yeah, no you're right. I just thought, I don't know...," she muttered, not really knowing what to say.

The cookies still looked like they spelled her name, even if Michaela couldn't see it. Michaela took the ginger snap that dotted the last 'i' in Paivi's name and grabbed a napkin.

"Come on, let's get some punch!"

Paivi grabbed a chocolate chip cookie and followed her over to the next table. An older lady in a Tartans sweatshirt, wearing a Scottish beret on her head ladled punch from a large bowl into red paper cups.

Paivi glanced into the bowl and felt sick. The fruit in the punch began to arrange itself into two words.

I KNOW

Paivi could hardly believe her eyes, but after the cookies she wasn't so surprised. She was scared. What did they know about her? And who knew it?

The woman stopped pouring and looked at Paivi.

"Are you feeling okay, sweetheart?" Her hand with the ladle was hanging just above the fruity words in the punch bowl. "You look like you've seen a ghost."

"No, no, I'm fine," she mumbled. Maybe the ladle would mess up the fruit. She stood there staring at the bowl, waiting. It broke the surface, breaking up the fruit letters. But after the lady served the next portion of punch, the fruit seemed to gravitate back together, like they were full of magnets. The words had reformed.

I KNOW

Michaela grabbed two cups of punch, said a quick thank you to the woman and led Paivi over to a table.

"Are you all right?" She sounded concerned. "You look like you're going to puke! Please don't puke on me, I really like this dress! But seriously, do you think you are sick from dinner or something? You know you are allergic to cheese." She looked around and dropped her voice to a whisper. "Or maybe this is because Jason is here with his girlfriend?"

Paivi's mind was racing. She couldn't tell Michaela. Paivi felt crazy herself, and she was sure Michaela would agree. She hadn't seen the words in the cookies or the punch.

"Here, maybe if you get some punch, you'll feel better." She pushed it towards Paivi.

She was afraid to look into the glass, for fear there would be some kind of message.

"Look, I'm sorry," she said, trying to sound normal. "I just don't feel well. You're right; it was probably all that cheese on the pizza. But it's cool, I'll be fine."

"Seriously? What was Miranda Swenson thinking, wearing that hideous yellow dress? She looks like Big Bird!" Michaela giggled as she nodded discreetly in Miranda's direction before shoving a cookie in her mouth. The table she chose had a perfect view of the people waiting in line for refreshments.

Paivi turned to look and snorted, hurriedly covering her mouth. The punch almost made a quick exit.

They didn't notice two girls walking up to the table. The first was short and plump and was dressed in orange, resembling a pumpkin. The other was somewhat skinny and wore a green dress.

"Hey," said Pumpkin, looking at Paivi.

"Um, hi?" Paivi tried to figure out if she should know the girl from somewhere.

"We're supposed to tell you that Christian Nelson

50

wants to talk to you," Green Bean explained.

"Who's Christian Nelson?" Paivi asked, although she was worried she might already know.

Pumpkin and Green Bean exchanged a look that clearly read 'what an idiot.'

"Everyone knows Christian. He seemed to think you'd know him too. Anyways, he's sitting over there." Green Bean gestured to the other end of the cafeteria, where a bunch of students were sitting at a table, talking and laughing. He was there, in the middle of the group. He wore sunglasses, so Paivi couldn't see his eyes, but she could see his blond hair, which looked white in the light, very clearly.

Her hands shook as she grabbed her used cup and napkin from the table.

"Come on Michaela, I wanna dance," she said, standing up abruptly.

"Whatever," said Pumpkin.

The girls, looking a bit annoyed, turned and headed back to Christian Nelson's camp.

"Don't you want to go over and talk to that guy? That's the one that was checking you out on the first day of school. He's pretty cute. And he looks pretty popular," Michaela said, pulling on her arm.

"I'm not interested. And I don't think he's cute at all," she added firmly. "I just want to go back to the dance floor. Let's go find the girls."

Paivi dragged Michaela back into the gym and disappeared into the throng. She had a hard time enjoying herself after the cookies and punch incident, and tried to make sure she was in the middle of the group as much as possible. She didn't want to have to deal with Pumpkin or Green Bean or any more of Christian Nelson's entourage.

She couldn't wait to go home. Who was making food talk to her? Could it have been Christian Nelson? She still thought she might be seeing things. And she didn't know who to talk to about it. Hopefully, it would be over now. She had made it quite clear that she didn't want to talk to him. Unfortunately, there was one small problem. Paivi would still be forced to see Christian every day at lunch and there was no getting around it. She shivered at the thought and tried to push it from her mind.

Chapter Six
All Hallows Eve

"Now can anyone tell us the positive aspects of globalization? Why is it a good thing?" Dr. Hasenpfeffer stood before the class. She was oblivious to the fact that most of the students in the class were not paying any attention to her. Some had snuck their headphones up through their sweatshirts and were listening to music. Some were passing notes. And some had even succumbed to a sweet mid-class slumber, brought upon by the consumption of too many Tartan burgers at lunch and the overly warm conditions in the classroom. Paivi turned to look at the clock and couldn't help noticing that Michael Giannotti was in such a deep sleep that he was emitting a snore every so often and a large puddle of drool was spreading slowly across his notebook, causing the few notes he had taken to run. She was astounded by Dr. Hasenpfeffer's lack of attention to this fact. She felt it was quite possible that the good doctor had just stopped caring whether they listened or not.

Paivi genuinely liked Dr. Hasenpfeffer, even if she had the worst case of scatterbrain Paivi had ever seen. She really felt her teacher was a nice lady. And when she wasn't captivating them with astounding tales of Clarence the cat and his habit of pishing all over her carpets, she did have interesting things to say.

Unlike the rest of her classmates, Paivi was not in a food coma, in fact, her stomach was twisted in knots of hunger because she still hadn't been to lunch yet. And even though she could see the future, she couldn't make it arrive any faster, so she figured she might as well say something. Besides, she was slightly bored and a little annoyed that she was surrounded by such lazy idiots. And she felt kind of sorry for Dr. Hasenpfeffer.

She raised her hand.

"Dr. H., globalization could be considered positive because it gives jobs to people in other parts of the world. That might give them more opportunities and maybe they would earn more money than before," she said.

Dr. Hasenpfeffer seemed surprised that someone had actually answered.

"That is correct Paivi. One could say it is also a positive for the consumer. Companies generally take their production offshore in order to reduce costs. This gives them more of a profit, but it also passes some savings along to the consumer."

Jason, paying attention to their discussion with interest, raised his hand.

"Dr. H., what about all of those toys that we get from China? I mean, I know they are cheaper than if they were made here, but lately they have all been found to contain lead paint. My aunt had to throw out all of my little cousin's Super-Bots last week. You should have seen him cry—I thought someone had died!"

"Yes, Jason, that is one of the negative aspects of globalization. If the toys are made in China, we have to trust that the Chinese companies will abide by U.S. laws. Unfortunately, they don't always check the toys coming over, and that is why you have seen toys from China being recalled every day. I've heard a rumor that Chinese-made toys are going to be banned and will all be sent back. Think of how that could affect what Santa Claus puts under the Christmas tree!" she said, tapping her head with piece of chalk.

The idea of no toys or gadgets for Christmas rousted a few of the sleeping and comatose students, and the remainder of class was spent arguing about where else they could get them and how people would deal with the prospect of Santa delivering gifts filled with socks and underwear.

As the bell rang and they left the classroom, Dr. Hasenpfeffer shouted their homework at them through the din.

"Please don't forget to watch the presidential debate on Sunday night! Who would you vote for and why! We will discuss on Monday!"

"I can just see it now," said Jason as they filed through the door, "parents buying Chinese-made Chuckling Charlies like druggies score drugs! Instead of drug dealers, there will be toy pushers hanging out at the playgrounds and on street corners!"

"Yeah, they will open their trench coats and instead

of watches, they will be lined with dolls and action figures!" Paivi pretended to be opening a coat, laughing. "Got your Soldier Steve toys, step right up!"

"So, any big plans for the weekend?" Paivi asked as she walked down to lunch with Jason.

"We're going to some Halloween party tomorrow."

"Oh, is it Amanda Montoya's party?" Her heart fluttered.

"I'm not sure. Probably. Melissa just told me we were going as Hansel and Gretel." He sounded a bit angry.

Paivi laughed.

"We're going, too! You sound less than enthused. I don't understand why! Lederhosen are one of the more attractive costumes a guy could wear!" She poked him in the side and snickered. "I haven't quite picked out what I'm wearing just yet."

"I just don't like being told what to wear and what to do," he snapped.

Paivi smiled inside. Maybe there was trouble in paradise. Her mind flitted to the thought of dancing with Jason at the Winter Dance.

"Oh, on Sunday, I guess I'll be watching the debate. Maybe we should have a Debate Party. I'll call Crystal and a couple of the others. We could order a pizza or something," she suggested.

"That sounds cool. Just let me know what's up. Dude, I'm starving." He patted his stomach with both hands. They were entering the cafeteria, their nostrils bombarded by the smell of burgers, fries and cookies. "I'll see you later!"

Paivi headed over to her table and dropped her bag onto her seat. She felt good today. It was Friday, which meant two days to sleep in. As an added bonus, she would get to see Jason two extra days. She was also excited because basketball tryouts were on Monday. Not that the practices were all that exciting, but the games would be great. She felt the good day warranted a nice big chocolate chip cookie. They served them hot in the lunch line, the chocolate still gooey.

"Are you going to get anything Mick?" she asked and grabbed a dollar from her wallet.

Michaela dug through her backpack and pulled out a small purse.

"Let's go. You're in a rather good mood today," Michaela said suspiciously.

"Yeah, I know! How could you not be! It's Friday, we're going to a Halloween party and basketball starts Monday." She tried to pull the doofy smile off her face before it gave her away.

"By any chance is Jason going to be at the party tomorrow?" Michaela asked casually, one eyebrow raised.

"Yes, but so is his girlfriend, so it's not like he's coming because of me," Paivi said with a pout. "But he seemed less than happy about the costumes Melissa wanted them to wear."

They shuffled a few feet forward in line. Paivi took a quick look around to make sure neither Jason nor his friends were around.

"She wants them to go as Hansel and Gretel!" she

whispered loudly.

Michaela snorted. "Well, I don't even know them very well, but I'm beginning to think they're not going to last very long!"

Paivi smiled. If only she could tell Michaela what she knew.

"And I invited him over for Sunday because we are supposed to watch the presidential debate for class. I'm going to invite Crystal and some others from class too," she added.

"Nice move! Ah, finally." They had made it to the front of the line.

Paivi followed Michaela through the lunch line, noticing the tater tots had arranged themselves into her name.

PAIVI

The green beans were apparently trying to get her attention as well.

I KNOW

She didn't even flinch at the sight of them this time. She continued with Michaela down the line, paid for her cookie and they headed back to their table.

In the weeks since Homecoming, Paivi had seen numerous messages and her feelings about them had moved from fear to mild annoyance. She saw the words spelled out in her colored pencils in her locker and in chalk dust on the chalkboards in her classes. On her way to and from school on the bus, she witnessed signs rearrange themselves as they passed. It had even appeared in her morning Cheerios from time to time. The words were always the same.

PAIVI

I KNOW

In fact, not only was she annoyed; she was getting more and more angry. She still kept receiving the icy stares from Christian Nelson day after day. She was convinced that he was somehow behind her strange messages, yet she wasn't quite sure she was ready to march over to his lunch table and punch him in the nose. Maybe she could just yell at him. A lot. But until that moment, she was content with returning his stare. She made sure when she did that it was equally icy and unfriendly. She might not be able to send him messages in his food, but she was NOT going to lose a staring contest.

The evening of the Halloween Party had arrived, and the air was cool and crisp. The leaves crunched under their feet as Paivi and Michaela walked up the ridiculously long driveway that led to Amanda Montoya's house.

Amanda's parents were well known in town. Mrs. Montoya was one of the top realtors in the area. There wasn't a house for sale in St. Andrew that didn't have her picture in the front yard. Her large, white SUV was covered with her picture and the logo of her real estate firm. Mr. Montoya owned a very successful chain of supermarkets called 'Alfredo's.'

The girls had known Amanda since their grade school years at Prairie View Elementary. They had been Girl Scouts together, and even though they didn't see her all of the time, she still invited them to all of her events.

Paivi and Michaela were always thrilled to go to Amanda's parties because a party at the 'Montoya Mansion,' as it they referred to it, was not to be missed. Amanda's parties always out-did all others. At Amanda's tenth birthday, her parents had ordered a small carnival to be set up in their huge back yard. There had been a Tilt-a-Whirl, a little roller coaster and a huge Ferris wheel, along with a ton of carnival games.

There was no telling what the Halloween party would have in store for them. Scattered throughout the front yard were real gravestones. Moss hung from their decrepit exteriors and there was a slight fog drifting among them, skimming across the dead leaves on the ground.

"Wow, Amanda's parents have really outdone themselves, if that is possible!" Paivi pulled her cloak a little closer around herself, trying not to shiver.

Paivi and Michaela had decided to dress as vampires. Cute vampires, not icky ones. They both had on long, crushed velvet dresses. Paivi's dress was a deep burgundy. She topped it off with a long black wig and a set of fangs. Michaela's dress was a deep purple. She didn't need a wig, as her hair was already long and dark.

"Ooo, come on, this is creepy!" Michaela grabbed Paivis arm, quickening her pace. As they neared the door, they passed one last gravestone, a pile of leaves lay at its base. Suddenly, the pile jumped off the ground and lunged at them.

"Uhhhhhh," it moaned, echoing through the front

yard.

The girls let out a blood-curdling scream and ran to the front door, knocking frantically. The leaf-creature was advancing on them. They started pounding on the door, screaming. The door creaked slowly open and the girls didn't bother to wait for an invite. They tumbled through the door, nearly falling over each other. They had not yet noticed the large figure standing before them. The sound of a chainsaw ripped through the foyer, the figure held the machine over its head. Its face was covered with a white hockey mask. The girls screamed again and fell into a heap against the front door.

At that moment, the light switched on, illuminating the foyer. Mrs. Montoya appeared, dressed in an elaborate witch costume. She carried a tray filled with goblets that were emitting a green smoke.

"Hi girls," she said, smiling in their direction. "Sorry about that." She gestured to the large figure next to her. "Honestly, Fredo, you are going to give these kids a heart attack!"

"Hi girls! We were just having a little fun, weren't we?" Mr. Montoya removed his mask. "Boy did we get you good!"

He laughed heartily.

"I take it you ran into Chase in the front yard." Mr. Montoya boomed as a leafy figure waved through the window next to the door. Chase was Amanda's younger brother.

Paivi and Michaela picked themselves up off the

floor and straightened out their costumes.

"Man, Mr. M., you had me scared out of my mind! That was crazier than the last haunted house I went to!" Paivi's heart was still pounding in her chest.

"Well, go on down, everybody is in the basement. Have fun!" he shouted, revving the chainsaw again.

Mrs. Montoya laughed and rolled her eyes. "Don't mind him!"

The girls followed her down the spiraling stairs into the basement. The Montoya's basement was hardly normal. It was considered a wing of their already expansive home. There was a full second kitchen, where Mrs. Montoya was setting down the smoking drinks.

"Here girls, try a 'Witch's Brew.' Amanda is down here somewhere." She emptied the tray and turned to leave. "Have fun!"

The girls leaned back against the counter of the bar and surveyed the scene. Music thumped from speakers hidden out of sight. A mix of popular and Halloween themed songs, including 'Monster Mash' and 'Thriller,' had a few people dancing.

In front of them was a huge recreation room. Off to one side, in front of a roaring fire, was a grouping of fluffy couches and opposite on the wall 'The Exorcist' played on a large movie screen. There were a number of costumed people lounging in the cozy corner.

With all of the costumes and make-up, it was hard for Paivi to tell who was who. She looked to see if Jason was over there, but she couldn't tell.

In the center of the large room was a pool table, where Dracula, Frankenstein, a hockey player, and a banana were in the middle of an intense game. Off to the side was a poker table, which at the moment was being used for a Ouija board. Candles were the only light on that side of the room. Paivi could hear gasps and shrieks as the crowd around the Ouija board read the messages it gave them. She could see Amanda, dressed as a mermaid, sitting at the table.

Beyond the table was a wall of windows with large French doors that led to a stone patio and fire pit. Paivi could see more people outside sitting by the fire, roasting marshmallows.

"Hey, let's go say hi to Amanda and then go out and roast some marshmallows before it gets too cold. I am absolutely dying for one!" Paivi wondered if Jason was outside.

Oh, stop it, she told herself. What is the point? He would be here with his girlfriend.

Anyways, maybe she would meet a cute guy at the party to tide her over until Jason and Melissa were no more; there were definitely plenty of them around!

"I love roasting marshmallows!" Michaela squealed.

They headed towards the group at the Ouija board.

"Is it bad when most of your marshmallows end up in the fire instead of in your mouth?" Michaela laughed.

They approached Amanda's chair, attacking her with hugs from both sides, careful not to crush her elaborate mermaid's costume.

"Hey!" She jumped up, turning around to hug them

both. "You guys look fabulous!"

"Uh, guys, I think the board has a message for Paivi," squealed one of Amanda's friends, Darcy. "Look, Marina is writing it down while it moves."

Darcy gestured to their hands on the small device gliding across the Ouija board.

"What did it spell out, Marina?" she asked.

"Just a second, I don't think it's done." Marina waved Darcy off, her eyes following the planchette eagerly.

Their hands continued to move with the device.

Paivi started to get nervous. What was it going to do, tell her I KNOW for the eightieth time?

"Okay! I've got it!" shouted Marina. "Oh my god, Paivi!"

Paivi could feel her heart start to sink.

"Paivi loves Jeff!"

"Who is Jeff? Is he here at the party?" asked a girl dressed like Princess Leia from Star Wars.

Paivi laughed and felt a sense of relief wash over her. "Jeff? I don't think I even know anyone named Jeff. I guess he'll just be my mystery man!"

The banana shooting pool had overheard the girls' conversation and raised his hand.

"Hey, my name is Jeff! Who loves me?"

They all laughed.

"According to the all-knowing Ouija, Paivi here does!" Amanda pointed her out. "Jeff, meet the new love of your life!"

"Nice!" He walked over to Paivi. "Hi, I'm Jeff the

banana. Damn glad to meet you!"

He pumped her hand in an exaggerated handshake. Paivi blushed.

"Hi Jeff the banana. It's a pleasure?!" She wasn't so sure.

"I'll be seeing you," he pointed his two fingers at her like pistols, pretending to shoot, blew the smoke off of them and winked, "later! But right now I've got to finish my game! Bye!"

Amanda turned to Paivi and Michaela. "Do you guys want to play? We can pull up more chairs."

"That's cool, we'll come play in a little bit. We want to go roast some marshmallows! Did you get stuff to make S'mores?" asked Paivi.

"Girl, you know I did! Hey, Michaela, try not to drop all of your marshmallows into the fire this time!" Amanda's laughter followed them out the door into the crisp evening.

Chapter Seven
A Most Unwelcome Guest

Amanda's backyard was a little cozier than the front, what without all of the gravestones, fog, and scary leaf monsters. The night was very clear, which made the yard bright, despite the moon only being at half strength. Paivi and Michaela walked towards the fire. There were already some partygoers seated on the outdoor couches, extending marshmallow-laden branches over the open fire. The flames crackled and licked the marshmallows, as if it wanted to eat them itself.

"Hey, where did you guys get those sticks?" Michaela asked.

"We had to go to the end of the yard, on the edge of the woods there." Pointed a guy dressed as a pirate. "Wait, do I know you?"

He flipped up his eye patch.

Michaela took a closer look, leaning towards the fire.

"Dave? Is that you? Oh my god, I haven't seen you in forever!" She moved closer to Dave the pirate, looking eager to continue the conversation.

Paivi took a look and didn't recognize anyone around the fire. There were no open spaces to sit. She set her witch's brew down on a nearby table and tapped Michaela on the shoulder.

"Hey, I'm going to run and get us some sticks, I'll be right back."

"Cool! Thanks, girl!" Michaela turned back to Pirate Dave.

Paivi took her time walking to the edge of the Montoya's backyard. It took her down a slight hill and ended at the edge of the woods. Off to the left was a small lake. In the distance she could see the lights of the other large houses that surrounded it. The moonlight left a thin silver path across the water.

Paivi could see two figures walking back towards the house from a path that wound around the lake. She could make out someone dressed as the Grim Reaper, carrying a large scythe and wearing a flowing black robe with a hood. A girl walking along side the Reaper wore her hair in a ponytail, a pink poodle skirt, and a letter jacket.

Interesting, she thought. Death and a bobby soxer.

She laughed silently to herself and pulled the hood of her cloak up around her head. She didn't really feel like talking to anyone. She turned back towards the trees, moving a little closer to them. In the shadows, she tried to spy some proper marshmallow-roasting sticks.

Paivi turned back towards the house to see how Michaela was getting on and found herself face to face with the Grim Reaper. She jumped slightly at the sight of the dark cloak with no face. The bobby soxer was gone. She could see her walking across the yard, back toward the group around the fire.

"Sorry, Grimmy," she chuckled, her hand pressed to her heart. "It's not my time yet!"

"I wasn't aware you were such a comedian," retorted a voice behind the black fabric that she didn't recognize. A black gloved hand pulled off the hood.

"You!" Paivi said, shocked to see the face of Christian Nelson. "What do you want?"

She took a step back towards the trees. She could see the house and bonfire in front of her, and wanted nothing more than to take off and head back to Michaela.

"Tsk, tsk," clucked Christian. "Why so unfriendly?"

She looked into his eyes. They shined brightly in the moonlight. She decided they weren't as scary up close. She didn't feel so much afraid as she did annoyed.

"Look, I just need to find a couple sticks and then I am going back to the fire." She turned back towards the trees. She noticed some sticks on the ground and could see her name spelled out in them.

PAIVI

Christian laughed.

She whipped back around.

"I knew it was you! Why? Why are you doing this? What do you want from me?" she demanded. She could feel the energy building up in her, but fought it. A scene in front of a group was something she couldn't risk.

"I have my reasons." He smirked and Paivi

contemplated slapping it clean off his face.

I could get away with it here, she thought, we aren't at school.

"Anyways, I've been trying to get your attention for awhile," he added.

"If you wanted to meet to me so badly, why didn't you just come up and talk to me like a normal person? That would have worked better than staring me down with the evil eye and leaving creepy messages in my food," she retorted.

He turned toward the pond, looking out at the sparkling water.

"I have a reputation to uphold. Christian Nelson wouldn't just go up and talk to someone, especially a freshman," he said smugly. "They all come to him."

"Well I am glad you think enough about yourself to refer to yourself in the third person. However, I could care less about you and your reputation. So if you don't mind, I'd like you to just leave me alone and forget whatever it is you think you know about me." She grabbed two sticks out of the piles that had spelled her name and turned to head back to the party.

He grabbed her arm and pulled her back. She tried to pull away, but he only pulled her closer.

"I don't think that's possible. You see, I know things that I just really can't forget." His face was so close to hers she could feel his breath.

Her eyes flashed with anger. Unable to hold back this time, she felt the energy rush out through her fingertips.

A strong wind rushed around them causing the twigs and leaves at their feet to dance, some clinging to the bottom of their cloaks. In an instant the air was calm once again. Christian seemed unfazed.

"Oh yeah, like what," she spat, holding her ground.

"Well," he looked into her eyes and smiled, "you're quite cute when you're mad. Has anyone ever told you that?"

She didn't answer.

"I know about you, Paivi; that you can see things. But I didn't know about this," he waved his arm at the mess of leaves and twigs that clung to him and began to pick them off. "You're more powerful than I thought. I also know about your parents, John and Maria. I know that your brother, Torsten, is not 'gifted', as you might say, like you and your parents."

"So what, what can you do about it? Are you going to tell people? Do you really think anyone would believe it?" she asked.

His eyes narrowed.

"Are you really willing to find out? Do you want to be labeled as a freak?" he hissed.

She wavered a little, but continued to hold his gaze.

"You wouldn't." She wasn't so sure of that. "How did you find out? All I know is if you know about me and you can send those messages, then you are just as 'gifted.' Why couldn't I just tell people about you?"

"Well, you could try, but no one at school wouldn't listen. Let's just say they all owe me something. Plus, they love me," he said, flashing a gleaming white smile. "They would never believe you, you're a nobody. And I can't tell you how I know, that's a secret, I'm afraid."

"So what is this all about then? What do you want?" she demanded, her voice rising.

"Look, you need to understand, right now—I own that school. I'm offering you an opportunity here to join me. Together we can have complete control of that place and everyone in it. Just think, you could be the most popular girl in school." He studied her face closely and released his grip.

"I don't care about that. I don't need to be popular. I don't want to have to manipulate people just to be cool. What if I say no? You'll tell everyone about my parents and me? Basically, you want to blackmail me to be your friend?" Paivi said, rubbing her arm.

"Ooo, blackmail is such an ugly word. Let's say encourage. Look, do you know anyone else who is special like us?"

"No." She took a step back.

"Well, there are a few others at our school, but they aren't even aware of what they have. They would think I was crazy if I tried to talk to them. They wouldn't understand. But haven't you ever just wanted to talk to someone about it, to not have to hide what you can do?" He moved closer to her. "Haven't you ever wanted a friend that you could be yourself around? Paivi, if those people knew about you, about us, we would be totally on our own. Outcasts. This way, at least we have some protection. Think of it this way, we'd be in this together."

"Well, I think you're nuts, but it's not like you're

giving me any choices here." She thought about it, looking back at the bonfire, back at the others. They were all so normal.

"Fine, Christian, fine. Whatever it takes to protect my family. But you have to give me some time. It's not like I am going to be your best friend overnight. And I am not going to manipulate people. I'll leave that to you."

"Okay, okay, you've got a deal. I knew you would come around!" he smiled and clapped his hands together.

"Can I go back to the party now?" The crisp air crept up her neck, sending a shiver down her spine. She pulled her cloak closer. It was colder than she thought.

Christian pulled his mask back down, concealing his face.

"Here, I'll walk with you."

"Gee, thanks," Paivi retorted sarcastically.

They quickly made their way across the yard, neither of them saying a word. Images swam before her eyes. Friends. Her parents. Jason. Her heart sank into the pit of her stomach. There was no way out of this.

The group on the patio had grown since Paivi had left to gather the sticks. Michaela was still in deep conversation with Dave the pirate. They were sitting on a bench together, close to the fire.

"Bye Paivi, I'll talk to you on Monday at lunch," said Christian quietly from behind his mask. He squeezed her arm and headed back into the house.

Paivi pulled her arm back, as if his touch burned her. She said nothing and turned her back to him. Excusing herself and squeezing through the crowd, she tapped Michaela on the shoulder with a stick.

"Oh, thanks P!" was all Paivi got out of her.

Great. Now she was on her own and there was still nowhere to sit.

"Paivi?" asked a familiar voice.

She turned around to find herself looking at a more pleasant view this time. Jason stood before her, dressed as a Chicago Cubs baseball player. Paivi smiled.

"Hi! What happened to the lederhosen, Hansel? I thought you'd look so cute! Think of how much leg you could show with those shorts!" she teased. "Where's Melissa?"

"Um," he looked down, fiddling with the leather mitt he was carrying, "we broke up."

She stared at him for a moment and hid her smile behind her hand. "Oh my god! I'm so sorry! Are you okay?"

Maybe this wouldn't be such an awful night after all, she thought.

Chapter Eight
The Debate

Paivi Anderson
Current Events p.6
Dr. Hasenpfeffer

 This week I read another article in the <u>St. Andrew Herald</u> by Jerome Knowles. It was called "The Final Debate: It's too late for Senator Stevens." He writes that Moira Kelly has already won the election. According to the polls, Kelly leads Stevens 64% to 46%. Knowles says it means Kelly will definitely win because in history very few candidates come back from that kind of margin. Kelly also has bonus points with voters because she got the head of the Righteous Front, Malcolm Davis, to agree to talks after the election. Knowles thinks only a miracle will save Senator Stevens and his campaign at this point. I am planning to watch the debate on Sunday because I think it will be interesting and because it is a class assignment.

   Paivi, enjoy the debate! B+
   Dr. H.

Into the Shadows

Senator Stevens sat in a chair in his dressing room. It was quiet. The hair and make-up people had just left, and none of his staff had returned from their tasks. There was still some time before the debate was to begin. He sat back in his chair and looked at his clean, smiling reflection in the mirror. He had never really been handsome as a young man, but now he at least looked distinguished. He looked like a...

A President, he finished the thought, taking a sip of water from a glass on the counter.

He adjusted his tie, which was unnecessary, as it was already perfect. He polished the American flag pin on his lapel and smiled.

This is it, he thought.

He got up from his chair and retrieved a small flash drive from his briefcase, tucking it into the pocket of his suit jacket.

The door to his dressing room opened and his assistant Martin appeared.

"They're ready for you, Senator," said Martin, holding the door.

Senator Stevens followed Martin down a hallway, which led to the large Auditorium Theater where the debate was to take place.

Chicago—middle America, where all of the average voters live, he thought.

The theater's large, lighted arches, painted a stunning gold, soared overhead. Colorful frescoes decorated the walls and ceiling.

A fitting place for my victory, he thought as they

entered the stage. Though the election wasn't until Tuesday, he knew it might as well be today.

"Senator." Jeff Clancy, one of America's most well known and respected newsmen walked up, extending his hand.

Senator Stevens reached out, shaking it heartily.

"Good to see you Clancy. How's the wife?"

"She's well, Senator. Truly, it is an honor to be working with you tonight! I think they are just giving us a chance to check out the surroundings," Clancy said, waving a hand at the expansive theater.

Stevens nodded.

"Well, I better be on my way, good to see you sir," he paused, looking back at the Senator, "good luck tonight!"

"Thanks." He didn't need luck. He had something more.

After visiting his podium and checking his microphone with the sound booth, Senator Stevens was led back to his dressing room to await the beginning of the debate. The next hour raced by, filled with last minute briefings and hair and make-up touch-ups.

And then it was time.

The Senator stood in the wings, listening to the cheers of the audience as Jeff Clancy was introduced. Jeff addressed the crowd briefly, and then they turned their attention to the stage. It was decked with bright red curtains against which hung long blue banners. Lines of white stars ran along the banners from floor to ceiling. Two podiums on the stage were decorated in a similar motif.

Senator Stevens could see the crowd behind the bright lights. A few butterflies bounced around his stomach, but he pushed the feeling aside.

This is it, he thought, can't get nervous now.

Jeff Clancy first gave the introduction of Stevens' challenger, the Liberal Party candidate Moira Kelly. She was quite popular and had run a good campaign. But Stevens knew even her great successes couldn't stand up to his plan.

"I would like to welcome Senator Wendell Stevens to the stage," announced Jeff Clancy.

There was applause, but not quite the same energy as when his opponent was introduced.

Senator Stevens walked across the stage and waved to the crowd, smiling. He made his way over to Moira Kelly and shook her hand.

"Good luck, Senator," she offered politely.

"Good luck to you as well," he replied, thinking she would need it more than him.

The debate began as the others had. Jeff Clancy provided the questions, giving Stevens and Kelly their last opportunities before the election to express their positions. There were questions on welfare, the environment, healthcare, and the economy.

At last it came.

"Our next question deals with our national security. Senator Stevens and Ms. Kelly, in light of the seemingly uncontrollable terrorist attacks across the nation, the public would like to hear what solutions you offer for this problem. Ms. Kelly, you may answer first."

"Terrorism is something we have been dealing with on a daily basis and it has touched everyone's lives. I myself lost my dear cousin Georgie in the Starbucks bombing this past June in Boston. He left behind a wife and three small children." She paused as her voice caught in her throat. Taking a deep breath, she pressed her hand to her heart and closed her eyes. A tear rolled down her cheek.

It was everything Senator Stevens could do to refrain from rolling his eyes. Moira Kelly had used cousin Georgie's demise to win herself countless points in the polls. He put a solemn look on his face in order to appear sympathetic as she continued.

She quickly regained her composure.

"I feel that the only way we are going to get anywhere is if we set up peace talks with the Righteous Front, or the RF. For years we have been fighting violence with more violence, and what victories have any of the monies spent on defense and intelligence gotten us? Just more innocent citizens killed. Terrorist attacks didn't stop, even after we destroyed one of their main camps in Montana. The terror continues everyday. It's time to go in a different direction and make an effort to end the violence once and for all. I have already secured a meeting with RF commander, Malcolm Davis, on December 1st."

The applause in the auditorium was not as loud as when she was introduced. Many people were still quite nervous that Moira Kelly's plan was not vigorous enough and doubted it could or would stop the terrorists.

"If you would, please, give us your response,

Senator Stevens," asked Jeff Clancy as the applause died down.

"Thank you, Mr. Clancy. For a long time, the United States has been dealing with the scourge of terrorism. In the beginning, the attacks were on a grand scale, hitting major targets to make a point, and did not happen very often. After the formation of the Righteous Front, the attacks have become increasingly more regular and employ tactics that have been used by Hamas in Israel, the IRA in Great Britain, and ETA in Spain. Now, every grocery store and every shopping mall are targets. We can't even keep our schools safe, as we saw in the Lincoln Elementary School bombing."

People in the audience lowered their eyes, somber at the thought of the loss of so many lives. The attack had occurred almost a year ago, when a group of terrorists overran and elementary school, and blew up not only the children inside, but had car bombs rigged in the parking lot that killed numerous parents as they flocked to the school to find out if their children were okay. 863 lives were lost that day in Topeka, Kansas.

"However, I propose a different path. Ms. Kelly may choose to negotiate with terrorists. I, on the other hand, refuse to negotiate with people whose only way to get a point across is to blow up innocent children."

The crowd roared to life. Members of the audience jumped to their feet, applauding, screaming. Some were even in tears.

So far, so good, he thought. He could feel the energy in the room.

This will be mine.

He continued.

"In the past few weeks, I have been working with some very reliable intelligence informants. I have received some valuable information, which will help in our fight against these terrorists. The intelligence suggests that there are people in these United States, our own citizens, who knew about these terrorist attacks, and have knowledge of future attacks. And yet they have chosen to keep this information to themselves. They have chosen not to speak, allowing innocent men, women and children, people like Ms. Kelly's own cousin George, to die horrible deaths which could have been prevented."

There were gasps and whispers throughout the crowd.

"In this day and age, silence is complicity, and at this point, should be punished as treason. These people have betrayed you, betrayed those who have been killed, and betrayed their country. Now, what I propose is a committee including the Senate, the State Department, the FBI, CIA, and the U.S. Army to deal with these Enemies of the State. This is so important to the nation's security that I chose to begin the committee before the election takes place, because I feel your safety is more important than your vote. However, if you do vote for me, as your Commander in Chief, I will be able to work towards punishing the traitors and eradicating the Righteous Front from our shores."

He pulled the small flash drive from his pocket.

"This contains a list of the traitors who live among

us. To prove just how dangerous these Enemies of the State are, let me share a few names with you. Monty Larkin, an RF lieutenant, who is currently in the federal prison in Leavenworth, Kansas for planning a bombing in Detroit last February, is on the list. Also on the list is Elizabeth Sanchez, an RF operative who is on the FBI's Most Wanted List for a bombing in Miami in last August. The remainder have been living among you, keeping their terrifying secret from the good citizens of this great nation. I feel it is our duty to begin identifying these people as soon as possible and take them in for questioning."

"This is preposterous!" shouted Moira Kelly. "If this is a matter of national security, as you say Senator, shouldn't you immediately turn it over to President Hartman?"

"Madam, as a member of the Senate, my committee will report directly to the President, of course. However, in order to protect the public, the committee must be hand selected to ensure that the information doesn't fall into the wrong hands. As the original recipient of the list, I already know who can and cannot be trusted."

The audience was silent, watching the exchange between the candidates.

"How do we know we can trust you, Senator Stevens?" Moira Kelly could hardly contain her fury.

"Well, obviously, Madam, if I were one of these traitors, I certainly wouldn't be trying to punish my own. Are you certain of your own status? You wouldn't happen to be on this list, would you?" Stevens shot her an analyzing glance.

81

Moira Kelly lost her cool at that point, charging across the stage at the Senator.

"How dare you accuse me of being a traitor, you filthy, slimy scumbag!" she screamed.

Members of the security staff and both candidates' staffers ran out to attempt to pull the two apart as Moira Kelly attempted to choke the Senator, but had no success fitting her small hands around his fat neck. She pulled her arm back, setting up to punch the Senator in the face as a security officer grabbed her around the waist. Jeff Clancy ran up on stage as the curtain fell on the melee.

"Well folks, this brings us to the end of this evening's debate. Please join us on 'Good Morning' tomorrow for a full analysis. And please, don't forget to do your duty as Americans and vote on Tuesday. Good night."

There was a stunned silence in the Anderson's family room.

"I don't know what just happened," said Crystal as she stared at the screen, her jaw dropped. "What was that all about?"

"He can't do that. Marking people as traitors! What evidence does he have? This can't be allowed by the Constitution!" Jason raved.

"Well, hopefully this whole thing will just blow up in his face. I can't wait to see who is on that list. It's probably all Liberal Party members. He'll just use it to get rid of people he doesn't like," speculated Paivi. "I guess this will give us something to talk about in Dr. Hasenpfeffer's class tomorrow."

Chapter Nine

Game On

Paivi's leg bounced anxiously through all of her classes, finally calming down when she arrived to Current Events. Only two more periods until basketball tryouts, not that she was worried. She was confident she'd easily make the freshman team.

She could hear the students whispering as she plopped down in her seat. Most of them hadn't watched the debate, which was bound to disappoint Dr. Hasenpfeffer, who seemed more frazzled than usual. She knocked an entire stack of tests off her desk, sending them flying in a flutter to the floor. A girl who sat near Dr. Hasenpfeffer's desk jumped up to help her pick up the mess.

When everything was in its place, Dr. Hasenpfeffer settled herself into her leather chair. Paivi noticed a large coffee stain down the front of her ruffled cream blouse and her hair was haphazardly pinned down by a large gold barrette on the top of her head.

"Good afternoon, class," she began, finally getting herself together. "Let's get right to it. How many of you honestly watched the debate, or at least saw some news coverage about it?"

Paivi looked around the room. Aside from her hand and those of the few students who had come to her Debate Party, very few others had done their homework.

"Now children, I could understand why you might not finish a worksheet, but seriously, this is an assignment that might just be helpful to you in real life." Dr. Hasenpfeffer sounded exasperated at their apathetic response.

Stefan Jarvis, a student who normally spent the class drooling into his sleeve, had his hand raised.

Dr. Hasenpfeffer looked to be in a bit of shock, pressing her hands to her heart. "To what do we owe your glorious contribution, Mr. Jarvis?"

"Well, I just wanted to, you know Doc, put in my two cents," he responded.

"By all means," she offered.

"Well, I just don't get what the big deal is. I mean, who cares about these old, rich politicians. It's always the same crap, isn't it? All they do is lie, cheat and steal. I can't vote now anyways, and even if I could, it doesn't seem like our votes count for anything."

"Well, Mr. Jarvis, I am sure you plan on attaining the wonderful adult age of eighteen?" queried Dr. Hasenpfeffer.

"Yeah, next year," he said with a smile.

"In that case, you should know what you're in for. You have to take driving lessons before they give you a driver's license. Perhaps you should take the time to learn more about politics before you can vote. Otherwise you have people voting for some idiot because he or she has cool hair!" She sucked in a breath, having expended all of her air on her rant.

"Okay, okay!" conceded Stefan. "You win!"

The class laughed.

"Those of you who deemed it uncool should be sad that you missed such a monumental debate. If anything, the most important part was not the debate at all!" She looked around the classroom. "Those of you who saw it, can you please tell the class about it?"

"The part about the list of 'Enemies of the State,' or the part where Moira Kelly tried to punch Stevens in the face?" asked Jason.

"Let's focus on this list. For those of you who missed it, Senator Stevens informed the nation that he has access to a list of people who he is referring to as 'Enemies of the State.' These people, according to the Senator, could have stopped terrorist attacks. Some of them are, in fact, terrorists. They formed a committee and will identify the people, who will be brought in for questioning. What do you all think about this?" she asked, glancing around the room.

A few hands went up.

"Ah, Mr. Jarvis!" Dr. Hasenpfeffer gestured for him to speak.

"I think if it's true that these people on the list helped terrorists, then they should be punished," Stefan said.

Paivi raised her hand.

"But Dr. Hasenpfeffer, is it constitutional to just

round people up because of some list? I mean, how do we know this thing is legit?" she asked.

"Legally, you can be charged with a crime of omission if you know the details of a crime that is at some point committed. Usually it's a misdemeanor charge, something pretty minor in terms of the law. But the punishment can be more severe if someone dies. They would have to prove that the person knew about the crime, and I am not quite sure we know how they plan on determining that," Dr. Hasenpfeffer explained. "But you are right, they won't release any information on where the list came from. I think they are all hoping we will put our trust in them."

"Hey, Dr. H., you're old, so you would be a better judge. Should we trust them?" asked Jason.

Dr. Hasenpfeffer pretended to be offended. "Old! Old! I am not that old!" she protested.

"I'm sorry, you know what I'm saying. You have more life experience!" laughed Jason.

"Ah, yes, I see. Well, my answer to you would be to always ask questions. It's your life they're making decisions about. Being informed is the best thing to do. But I have to admit, I am nervous about this list. No good has come from singling people out. If you think back to some historical examples, there was the McCarthy Era in the 1950s when Communists were rounded up and harassed. We could even make comparisons to the Holocaust and the roundups of the Jews during World War II. But I would hope our government remembers the lessons learned during those times," Dr. Hasenpfeffer said.

The class was still discussing the debate as the bell rang and they exited the classroom.

"I wish we were older and we could vote, or at least be able to do something. If people let the government get away with this, its just insanity!" raved Jason as they made their way down the hall.

"Maybe it'll be okay," said Crystal. "I mean, if it really does stop the terrorist attacks, I don't know, maybe it'll be worth whatever trouble it causes."

"See! That's exactly it—selling out your freedom for your security!" Jason snapped back. Crystal's face fell.

"All right you two, save it for class tomorrow," said Paivi, pulling Jason toward the cafeteria. "I'll catch you later Crystal."

She turned to Jason. "Look, clearly you feel strongly about this, but you aren't going to get people to see it your way if you yell at them!"

"Don't you feel the same way I do, Paivi? I didn't peg you for a sheep." His words were sharp.

"I'm not a sheep! But nothing has even happened yet. Besides, what can we do? The election is tomorrow. Let's hope that the people who do have a say will do something about it. Until then, relax!" She spun angrily on her heel, looking over her shoulder and stuck out her tongue.

Paivi joined Michaela at their lunch table.

"What's his problem? He looked really mad," observed Michaela as she dug through her gigantic purse, looking for her wallet.

"Ah, he's just mad about that debate last night. You

know, politics and all that, nothing you would find too exciting," she said, watching Jason across the room at his lunch table, still sporting a sour look.

"You are right about that, sister," Michaela said, finding the wallet. "Let's go. I am starving! I hope they have my favorite M&M cookies today! Yum!"

As they made their way through the line, Paivi could see the tater tots arranged in a message.

SEE ME

Ugh, she thought.

Christian really seemed to have a thing for leaving her messages in food. Couldn't he just write her a note, or better yet, talk to her like a normal person?

After she had finished her lunch and Michaela was engaged in a very serious conversation over which football player at the next table was the hottest, Paivi excused herself and made her way over to Christian's table. He noticed her walking over, and told the guy next to him to move. He patted the seat, indicating to Paivi that she should sit.

"Gee, thanks," she said sarcastically. "So, you wanted to see me?"

"Yeah, we need to get together this week, I was thinking Wednesday at Al's Café," he said, not waiting for an answer.

"I hate to break this to you, but I start basketball today and I have practice every day this week after school. There's no way my mom will let me go out on a Wednesday night," Paivi responded.

"What about Saturday, then?" Christian asked

through a mouthful of tater tots.

"Yeah, I guess Saturday would be alright, but it would have to be in the afternoon," she answered.

"So, Saturday it is. Al's, two o'clock." Christian looked satisfied. "Have you had any good dreams lately?"

He smiled.

"Very funny," she said. "And no, I haven't. See you Saturday. And by the way, I do have a phone." She grabbed a tater tot off his plate and held it up to him before popping it into her mouth. She stood up and headed back to her table, not looking back.

Paivi's first day of basketball tryouts had gone very well. She'd hit a few good shots and done everything the coaches had asked. At the end of the tryout, she was sore and all her muscles ached, but it was a good ache. She was pretty satisfied with her effort. Paivi went to bed early that night, completely worn out. Her head barely hit the pillow before she drifted off into a deep sleep.

Suddenly, she was walking down the hallway at school. She looked down and noticed she was dressed for practice. She entered the large gym, where groups of girls were practicing out on the basketball courts. The freshman team coach, Ms. Jensen, was talking with the head coach, Mrs. Espinosa. They both turned to her as she walked up.

"I was just telling your coach that I'm afraid we're going to need you on varsity," Mrs. Espinosa patted Paivi on the shoulder. "My center just quit on me. I've seen you play. You look perfect for the job. Now, I know it's a lot to ask, and it'll be rough in the beginning, getting used to the speed of varsity. Are you up for the challenge?"

"Oh my god, yes! Of course!" Paivi could hardly get the words out; she was so excited.

The picture changed. There was a man standing on a stage, but she couldn't see his face. Music played and confetti fell from somewhere up above. People cheered loudly, waving signs bearing the name 'Stevens.'

Paivi awoke suddenly with a gasp. She rolled over and checked the clock. The neon green numbers showed 2:37. The house was still, silent and dark.

She smiled to herself. She was going to be on varsity! She had thought she would make the freshman team, but varsity! This was unbelievable! She hugged the nearest teddy bear, Mr. Stinky. She lay back down and rolled onto her side, snuggling into her pillow. Her mind fell briefly on the other vision.

So the jerk wins, she thought. Maybe Crystal wasn't half wrong. Maybe the guy could at least stop the terrorists.

Paivi pushed the thoughts to the back of her mind, closed her eyes, and drifted off into a peaceful sleep.

The election came and went the following week with Senator Stevens winning in a landslide. Aside from Dr. Hasenpfeffer's lively classroom discussions on the topic, life returned to its usual concerns.

Paivi was more focused on basketball than anything else. It was a few days before Coach Espinosa offered her a spot on the varsity team. Paivi was relieved, but also nervous. She liked the girls on the freshman team and she didn't know any of the girls on varsity.

Friday was her first day of practice with the varsity girls. She had tried to take everything in but there was so much to learn. The girls were working so hard; there wasn't much time for socializing.

Paivi found herself paired with Leyla Bianchi, a junior forward, for a particularly challenging drill. Paivi had to turn her back to Leyla, and then pivot around to catch a pass. Leyla was supposed to tell her to turn to the right or left and then throw the ball, which should meet her as she turned.

"Left," Leyla called out, her voice echoing through the gym.

Paivi swung to the left, but before she could complete her turn, there was an explosion of pain in her face as the basketball crashed into her nose. She flew straight backwards onto the floor.

"Oops!" Leyla giggled, covering her mouth with her hand. Shay Montgomery, the team's point guard, joined her.

Her face throbbed making it difficult to open her eyes. Blood dripped down from her nose and pooled into her cupped hand.

"Paivi, are you bleeding?" Coach Espinosa ran over. "Off to the trainer's, let's go."

She helped Paivi up and pointed to the door of the gym. Paivi looked back to see Leyla still talking to Shay and laughing. Paivi glared at them and turned her back as she headed to the training room. She felt the energy building up again, her anger forcing it through her. She made no attempt to control it this time. In the gym the girls let out a shriek as a light bulb burst, raining glass onto the hardwood floor.

This is just the beginning, she thought to herself, trying to keep the blood from running onto the floor.

Saturday morning's practice was still unpleasant, but at least it was not as physically painful. Her nose still ached from the day before, and her eyes were slightly black underneath, but Paivi didn't want it to look like she was weak, or worse, afraid of Leyla, so she tried not to shy away from any of the drills.

Leyla Bianchi didn't throw a ball in Paivi's face, but she made her presence known. When Leyla picked teams for a scrimmage, she chose Paivi for her team, and then never put her into the game. When Coach Espinosa noticed and subbed Paivi in, Leyla made sure she never got the ball. Paivi could see she had no supporters on the team. Leyla had a group of about five girls that stuck to her like glue and the other teammates just ignored her.

She was glad when practice was finally over. She found that she was dreading meeting Christian less than she was dreading Monday's practice. It was a sunny November day and unseasonably warm. Paivi decided to walk downtown—it was easier than trying to explain to her parents who she was meeting. She didn't want to tell a complete lie, so she told her mother that she was meeting Michaela at Al's Café. It was the right place, just not the right person. Besides, she didn't mind walking when it was so nice out. She felt a bit cagey and figured some fresh air would do the trick.

As she walked through the neighborhood, she looked at the houses as she passed. Every house looked slightly different, one story, two stories, red, brown. Most were neat and tidy. Some were a bit run down and looked out of place.

As she turned on to Grove Street she stopped in front of a large Victorian house. It was known as the Butterman Mansion and it was by far Paivi's favorite house in all of St. Andrew. The imposing three-story mansion sat in a large garden surrounded by an ornate wrought iron fence. The house had been expertly painted in shades of purple and blue, accenting the delicate woodwork that made it resemble a gingerbread house. With a sigh, she crossed over a busy street into St. Andrew's downtown.

Al's Café was located in an old two-story brick building that dated from 1871. It was located in St. Andrew's historic downtown and overlooked the Fox River. Paivi opened the heavy wooden door and heard a jingle. The girl standing behind the register looked up from a magazine she was reading.

"Hi! Welcome to Al's. How many?" she asked with a smile.

"Hi, I'm meeting a friend." Paivi paused as she scanned the downstairs dining room. There were a few couples sitting at the tables, but no Christian.

"Blond guy?" asked the girl.

Paivi nodded.

"He's upstairs." She pointed to a staircase to the left.

"Thanks!" Paivi went around a corner and headed up a wide wooden staircase. As she entered the room, she could see Christian sitting at a table next to the fireplace and in front of one of the large windows. The room was large and airy with high ceilings framed by elaborate wood trim. A fire crackled in the stone fireplace, throwing shadows along the walls.

Aside from Christian, the room was nearly empty except for a table of three very loud middle-aged ladies sitting at the far end of the room and one very bored looking waitress.

Christian glanced up from the menu he was looking at, his face brightening.

"Hi!" he said. "Did someone mug you on the way over? Those are some nice black eyes."

"Funny." She took off her coat, hanging it on the back of the chair. "It's from practice. Apparently my teammates don't like me very much. Well, one, anyways."

Paivi had been too embarrassed to tell her parents about the incident with Leyla. She figured getting her parents involved wouldn't make the girls on the team like her any better.

"Really?" He raised an eyebrow. "Which teammate in particular?"

"Right, like you're really interested. What are you going to do, leave her a nasty message in her green beans?" she snapped.

"Look, I know we've started off on the wrong foot," he began.

"You think?" She leaned back, folding her arms across her chest and narrowing her black eyes.

"I want to make it up to you. If you tell me her name, I'll make sure that after Monday, she won't bother you again and everyone on the team will be nice."

"I want to know what you're going to do, first. I don't want this getting any worse." She touched her nose gingerly. "I don't need any more black eyes."

"Can you just trust me?"

"Um, so far, no," Paivi replied.

"If I can do this though, then maybe you can trust me?" He played with his silverware.

"Maybe. A little. But why won't you tell me anything?" She sat back, folding her arms over her chest.

"Let's just say, I have ways of taking care of it, and no one will know but me and this other person. In order to do that, however, I would need a name."

The waitress approached the table, pen and pad in hand.

"What can I get for you?" She tapped her pen on the pad.

"I'll have an Oreo shake please," answered Paivi, without looking at the menu. It's what she always ordered at Al's, they were famous for their shakes.

Christian ordered a cheeseburger and a chocolate shake. The waitress headed off to put in their orders.

"So, are you going to give me her name?" Christian asked.

"Alright, Leyla Bianchi. She's a junior," she

answered, fiddling with her napkin. She had mixed feelings about this. She wanted Leyla to leave her alone, but she wasn't sure she wanted Christian to feel like he had won her over.

"I'll take care of her on Monday. I know who she is and it won't be a problem. By practice everything should be fine." Christian was visibly pleased with himself, smiling like a Cheshire cat.

Paivi felt a little uncomfortable.

"Uh, thanks?" It sounded more like a question.

There was a loud burst of cackles from the table with the three ladies. Paivi jumped a little, she'd forgotten they were there.

"Now, I have a favor to ask you," Christian began. "I need you to tell me who is going to win the big football game next weekend between Chicago and Green Bay, and the exact score."

Paivi looked at him with a confused look on her face.

"What? How am I supposed to do that?"

He looked at her, raising an eyebrow.

"Okay, okay, I get why you asked me, but I can't do that. I've never had any dreams about that kind of stuff. I mostly have dreams about myself, or family and friends," she explained.

Christian looked up as the waitress approached, carrying their shakes and his cheeseburger.

"Here you go, Oreo shake." The waitress set the tall glass and metal tumbler carrying the freshly mixed shake in front of her. "Cheeseburger and chocolate shake. Enjoy!"

Paivi didn't waste any time digging in.

"So, let me guess, you've never really used your ability before?" he asked, taking a bite of his cheeseburger.

"Used it? I've just seen lots of things. They just come to me," she answered through a spoonful of Oreo shake.

"Exactly. No one has ever taught you to use your ability though." Christian popped a french fry into his mouth. "I've met other people like you. They could just turn it on and off. So try that and see if you can find out about next weekend's game."

"Okay Mr. Know-It-All, how do I even begin to do that?" Her spoon was paused mid-way from the cup to her mouth. "And why aren't you asking these other people to do this for you?"

A shadow passed across his face, and Christian met Paivi's gaze across the table.

"I don't want to talk about it." He looked away and continued. "Anyways, when they wanted to see something, they would concentrate on a person or event, and if they concentrated on it hard enough, they could see it. I've seen people do it, they kind of looked like they were meditating, you know, like Buddhist monks do."

"And they didn't have to be asleep?" Paivi was listening intently. She had never realized she could control it, her parents hadn't told her that part. Is it possible they didn't know?

"Nope, they could do it any time they wanted. The

reason you see the things you do in your dreams is because you have thoughts of those people or events in your subconscious. You were concentrating on them without even realizing it," he said matter-of-factly.

"Wow," was all Paivi could say. She stirred her shake with the spoon.

"What are you going to do? Bet on the game or something?" she asked.

"I won't worry you about that. The less you know the better. If I remember right, that's how you wanted it to be," he answered.

"But what if it doesn't work? What if I can't see the game?" She set her empty glass to the side.

"Well, you've got all week, I just need to know by next Saturday. You'll get it, don't worry." Christian pushed his empty plate forward.

He waved for the waitress to bring the bill. She hurried over with the check, handing it to Christian. Paivi took out her wallet, but Christian held up his hand.

"My treat," he said, opening his wallet, which was full of cash.

"Uh, thanks. I didn't realize you were Mr. Moneybags. Where did you get all that cash?" she teased.

"That's for me to know." He threw down some bills on the table. "Come on, let's go."

They made their way down the stairs to the entrance. Paivi put on her coat.

"See you at school on Monday, I guess."

"Do you need a ride?" he asked, scanning the street.

"No, thanks, I don't live far and it's not too bad out. I think I'll walk." She didn't want to explain to her parents why some strange guy was dropping her off.

"Ah, here's my ride. Later, then," he said, giving her a quick wave.

A black SUV pulled up to the curb. Paivi turned to head towards home, thinking about what Christian had told her. She walked quickly, barely taking in her surroundings. She wanted to get home and see if she could really choose what future to see.

Chapter Ten

Lists

Paivi Anderson
Current Events p.6
Dr. Hasenpfeffer

 This week's article by Jerome Knowles 'Election Upset!' from the <u>St. Andrew Herald</u> discussed the election results. President-Elect Wendell Stevens was elected in a landslide victory after revealing his new plan for dealing with the Righteous Front during the final debate. The voters are now waiting to hear when the Anti-Terrorism Coalition will take effect and the list will be released. Knowles states that the election was by far one of the biggest surprises in history. Personally, I am still surprised that Moira Kelly didn't win, because everyone seemed to like her. I hope that President-Elect Stevens' plan really does work and they get the terrorists off the street. I am sure most Americans would be happy to have no more attacks from the Righteous Front. People could go to work and school and never have to worry about dying and that would be an awesome change.

   Paivi, let's hope you're right! A- Dr. H.

Election Day was a happy blur for Senator Wendell Stevens, or rather President-Elect Stevens. Hand shaking, speeches, posing for pictures.

Sitting quietly in his office the next day, he could hear the hustle and bustle in the hallways. Government was going on all around him. He was happy to finally get some time to himself.

President-Elect Stevens glanced at the newspapers on his desk, a large picture of himself on the cover, with confetti and red, white, and blue balloons all around him. His hands were raised, fingers forming victory signs.

It was everything he had always wanted. He was now the most powerful man in the world. He leaned back in his leather chair. Soon enough, he would leave his small, cramped senator's office behind for his new place, the Oval Office in the White House. He closed his eyes, picturing himself sitting behind the large presidential desk in the Oval Office.

He sat forward suddenly in his desk, breaking his daydream. He felt like he had to check on it again. He pulled open the desk drawer, moved some papers aside, and slid a secret panel in the bottom of the drawer aside. He pulled an oddly shaped key from his pocket. It was a thin skeleton key with a tiny pyramid at the end. It wasn't smooth, but instead carved with various notches of different sizes and shapes.

Stevens remembered receiving the key from the office's previous tenant, Senator Reginald Tuttle. Tuttle said it had been passed to him some forty years before from the legendary Senator John Graham. No one knew when the key had been made.

He placed the odd-shaped key into the lock in the desk drawer. It clicked and popped open. There, in a velvet-lined compartment, lay the flash drive. The list. The future.

It made him a bit nervous, keeping something so valuable, so precious, in such an old-fashioned device. Luckily, both Senators Tuttle and Graham were long dead, leaving him as the sole person alive that knew about the key and the secret compartment in the desk.

In a week, he was to meet with his new committee, and the lists would go public. Then security wouldn't matter.

He thought about the names on the list. Some of his own family members were on there. Cousin Lisa, his nephew Danny. There had been others as well, his own assistant Martin, members of Congress, mayors, governors, and celebrities. He would approach them after the committee meeting. Perhaps by pledging their allegiance to the cause, along with a considerable cash donation, he could convince the committee to put them on the 'compliant' list. That should keep them out of trouble. But he would still keep an eye on them all. Just in case. It was clear that they could not be trusted.

There was one name on the list, however, that he would be sure received no special treatment.

It brought him back to his college days. Wendell Stevens had a difficult time in school. He found high school relatively easy, but upon entering Harvard University, he struggled in every class, spending all of his waking moments with his nose stuck in a book.

Wendell's obsession with studying, in addition to his frumpy and unattractive appearance, put a damper on his social life. It was, in a word, non-existent.

His roommate, Peter Farmington, was anything but awkward. He was tall and blond, good at sports and even better with the girls. It always irritated Wendell that Peter did so well in school, considering that they shared a room and Wendell rarely witnessed Peter crack a book.

Peter was never mean to Wendell. He even invited Wendell to a few parties throughout the year that they lived together in the dorms. They never had any disagreements or misunderstandings. Peter was an easy roommate and was liked by all, even Wendell, though he hated to admit it. In general, most of the other guys on their floor would have said Peter and Wendell were good roommates.

Deep down Wendell thought it was all so unfair. Peter had it all, looks, friends, brains, girls, and a fantastic personality. To Wendell, that made it even worse. He wanted to hate Peter, but he was just so darn nice.

Wendell only had to suffer with Peter's perfect nature for a short time. Peter Farmington dropped out of Harvard University during his sophomore year. He started a small company making computers out of his parents' garage with a couple of friends.

Today, Peter Farmington was the head of Vantage Tech, the world's most popular and influential computer company. Peter was the world's second richest man, behind some prince from the Middle East.

Into the Shadows

He had seen Peter Farmington many times throughout the years at dinners, cocktail parties, and various other functions. Peter was still just as charming and popular as he had been that year at Harvard. He always greeted him warmly.

All along it grated at him. Here was the world's most perfect person, popping in and out of his life, just to remind him that no matter how hard he tried, he could never be as friendly, successful, or all-around perfect as Peter Farmington.

But now to have seen that name on the list, could it be that Mr. Farmington was a fraud? Was his entire life a lie? He was sure it had to be. Soon enough the world would know that they had all been taken by this swindler.

President-Elect Stevens leaned back in his chair, cracking his knuckles.

I may not be the world's golden boy, he thought, but I am the world's most powerful man. Peter Farmington's time has come to an end.

Chapter Eleven
A Star Is Born

Butterflies crashed around inside Paivi's stomach. St. Andrew High School was hosting the biggest girls' basketball tournament in the area, and her team had made it to the championship game. The night before, Paivi had a vision that showed people cheering for her, but she was unable to see the events that led up to it. She woke up briefly and tried concentrating really hard on the game, like Christian had told her, but it didn't work. She was a little nervous about her abilities as well. She was supposed to tell Christian the score of the Chicago-Green Bay game tomorrow, and she still hadn't had any luck there, either. She had been a bit preoccupied with the tournament all week and in addition to that, her mind had been clouded with thoughts of Jason.

Maybe tonight after the game, I can focus a little more, she thought.

As she sat in her Math class, she thought back to Monday. Jason had come to her locker that morning, looking a bit sheepish.

"Hey, Paivi, I, uh, I wanted to apologize for getting

so mad the other day about the election," he had said.

Paivi had given Jason the cold shoulder the entire week before. When Senator Stevens actually won the election, Jason fell into such a funk that Paivi didn't dare talk to him. Besides, she felt he still owed her an apology and she wasn't about to give in, as much as it pained her to avoid him.

"It's about time." She gave him a dirty look.

"Please don't be mad," he pleaded. "I had to suffer the whole weekend because you weren't talking to me. I've been punished enough!"

"I just don't know if an apology will be enough to win me over," she added playfully. "What else have you got?"

"I know you have three games this week, what if I came to watch you play?"

Paivi was thrilled, but she couldn't show it, she had to keep playing the game.

"That's pretty good, but it did take you until Monday to apologize. That means you were a super sourpuss for almost a whole week." She straightened some items in her locker that were already straight.

"Wow, you drive a hard bargain, Miss Anderson. Okay, what if I throw in a movie on Saturday night. Your choice. I'll even go to," he gave a loud sigh, covered his eyes and whispered, "a chick flick."

Paivi slammed her locker and turned to face him. It felt like they were the only two people in the crowded hallway.

"Mr. Santos, I am impressed! That's quite the offer! I think I can live with that. Apology accepted." She held out her hand to Jason and shook it. Her fingers tingled as their hands touched.

"See you later in Current Events," she struggled to get the words out.

A movie with Jason...could the day get any better? she thought, turning in a daze, and running smack into Christian Nelson. Her heart dropped a little.

"Are you sure he's not your boyfriend? You are with him and awful lot."

"No," she answered curtly. "I don't have a boyfriend. He's just a friend."

"Just a friend? Right. Whatever. Anyway, any luck with those scores yet?" He walked next to her as she moved down the hall towards her biology class.

"No, not yet, but I'm working on it. I promise. See you later!" she added hurriedly as she dashed away from him through the classroom door just as the bell rang.

Paivi blinked her eyes, waking from her daydream. Mr. Patel was still going over the same problem on the board with the class. At least she hadn't missed much. She had a sick feeling in the pit of her stomach. What if she couldn't get those scores? What would Christian do? Paivi rubbed her eyes and tried to focus on the problem. She was letting all of these things cloud her mind when she should really be focusing on the game tonight. Everything else would just have to wait until later.

Paivi picked at her dinner, swirling the peas around the plate with her fork.

"Mom, Paivi didn't eat her peas," Torsten shouted to Mrs. Anderson, who was already cleaning up the kitchen. "Tell her she can't go to her game unless she finishes her peas!"

"Shut up, Tor!" She flung a pea at him from her plate.

"Mom! Paivi is throwing peas at me!" he screamed.

"Torsten, mind your own business, Paivi, stop throwing peas. Honestly, how old are you two? I could swear your kindergarten graduations were a long time ago!" said Mrs. Anderson, coming to the table to grab a few dirty dishes. "Now hurry up and get your stuff together or we will be late to the game. Your father is meeting us there when he gets off work."

"Mom, Torsten is trying to look pretty for the high school girls 'cause he thinks he's going to get a date. Look at all that gunk in his hair!"

Mrs. Anderson walked up next to Torsten's chair, inspecting his overly-moussed hairstyle. She wrapped her arms around him in a big bear hug.

"Of course my little Torsty is so pretty. He's just darling! What girl wouldn't want to go out with him?" She squeezed his cheeks. Torsten, still wrapped in his mother's embrace, turned to Paivi and stuck out his tongue. "So handsome, my baby boy!"

Paivi looked on in horror, her eyes and mouth open wide. "I think I'm gonna be sick!"

"Come on now, get your stuff and get into the car, we've got to go!" Mrs. Anderson rushed them out of the kitchen. "Paivi, make sure you have all of your things for the game."

Paivi rifled through her bag again quickly. Shoes, two pairs of knee-length white socks, ponytail holders, water bottle. Check, check, and check. She had already checked the bag three times before. She always felt her game was off if she forgot something. She knew it was all stupid superstition, but she didn't care.

As they drove through St. Andrew, they passed the First National Bank. Out front stood the bank's sign, which showed the time and temperature. Paivi was surprised to see what was not the time or the temperature.

GOOD LUCK PAIVI

She blinked and looked again, but all she saw was the lights showing 5:42 PM.

She half smiled at the thought of the message, but stopped herself. She couldn't start getting sucked into Christian's game. He was using her. He just wanted her to like him so he wouldn't feel so guilty about what he was doing. She was impressed to think that he might actually feel guilty about something, but she wasn't going to let him win that easy.

The school parking lot was already packed with cars when they arrived. Paivi said a quick goodbye to her mother and brother and made her way downstairs to the girls' locker room. After getting dressed, the team headed down the hall away from the gym and the crowds. Coach Espinosa and their assistant coach, an extremely thin man that went by the name of Chubby, waited for them in a classroom at the end of the hall.

The faces around the room were serious, solemn. Game faces. Coach Espinosa felt that if you were smiling, you weren't thinking about the game. The girls were all about business and listened intently while Coach Espinosa went over what plays and players to watch for. She began to go through the line-up. Missy, Elena, Gina, Leyla, and...Paivi?

Paivi looked up with a start at Coach Espinosa, a bit bewildered. She was starting? Her palms started to sweat.

"Paivi, Buffalo Glen is playing their usual center, Brooke West. I want you to guard her and only her. Paivi can't help anyone else tonight. And you all should double-team on Brooke any time she gets the ball. Don't leave Paivi alone. She is just as big and strong as Brooke, but Brooke has a lot of experience and she can score. She averages twenty-five points a game. If we are going to win tonight, we have to make sure she doesn't get those twenty-five points. Clear?" Coach Espinosa asked.

"Yes coach!" they shouted back in unison.

Coach Espinosa looked directly at Paivi.

"Remember, Brooke is all yours and make sure she does NOT score."

Paivi narrowed her eyes, focusing on her task. She nodded her head.

"Got it coach."

The girls made their way upstairs, chanting 'Tartans'

as loud as they could until they reached the door of the gym for warm-ups. They waited in the doorway until the music started, the beats echoing through the entire gymnasium. They ran in one after the other and then split into two lines, running around the court and slapping hands with fans in the crowd.

When the music stopped, the girls returned to the bench and the starters were seated. As they were introduced to the crowd, they made their way to center court to shake hands with their opponents and then returned to their bench.

At last it was time for the jump ball. Paivi went to center court. She balanced on the balls of her feet, knees bent, arms up. Her body was tense, she felt like a lion, ready to pounce. Brooke West stood inches away, in a similar stance. They looked at each other for a second until the referee presented the ball. Their eyes were glued to the prize.

"Ready?" the referee asked.

Paivi felt like she was going to explode.

The whistle blew—the referee threw the ball straight up in the air.

Paivi shot up like a rocket, going for the ball. Two hands on it, she pulled it down towards her and passed it off to one of the guards. Leyla Bianchi scored the first points for the Tartans.

The game continued at a quick pace. Paivi stuck to Brooke West like glue, struggling and shoving on both ends of the floor. Brooke managed a few shots over her, but not without receiving a few bruises. By the fourth quarter, Brooke West had given up. Every time she turned, Paivi was there. Every move to the basket caused her to get tangled in two or three Tartans. The Buffaloes were frustrated but had stayed in the game, always keeping within at least five points.

As the time wound down, the Buffaloes had a burst of energy, shooting a three-pointer and making a quick shot off of an out-of-bounds play to tie up the game. The Tartans couldn't get a shot in the final second and the game ended in a tie, forcing the game into overtime.

The girls returned to the bench to regroup.

"Keep fighting in there, Paivi, you're doing great. Guys, we need some good shots, quickly. Come on! Run your offense and stay on your toes. Let's go!" Coach Espinosa shouted.

Paivi looked up at the scoreboard and instead of the score showing a tie of 65-65, she saw the lights rearrange to spell out something else.

GOING FOR 3

And on the other side was one number.

15

She turned to look into the crowd, trying to quickly scan for Christian's face. There wasn't enough time, the buzzer rang and they were pushed back onto the floor.

Her mind was racing. Number 15 was going to go for a three. But if she did anything about it, she would be cheating, wouldn't she? They were lining up for the jump ball. There wasn't time to think. Elena had number 15, but there was no way to tell her now.

Focus, just focus, she thought, forcing herself to

look at the ball and get into position for the second jump ball of the game.

The referee threw the ball between her and Brooke West and they jumped. They both touched the ball, tipping it sideways into the hands of one of the Buffaloes.

The teams took off down the floor towards the basket. The Buffaloes took their spots on the floor, setting up their next play.

I have to do this, thought Paivi, scanning the floor for number 15.

The girl was coming in her direction, off a pick set by one of her teammates. Paivi saw the ball being passed to the short blond, who had set up out by the three-point line. She took her chance, leaving Brooke West unguarded, which she was sure to get in trouble for, but she didn't care.

The ball was almost to number 15, who didn't even notice Paivi approaching. Paivi got one hand on the ball and slapped it out of her hands, towards the other end of the floor and chased after it. The crowd erupted in cheers as everyone jumped to their feet. It was exhilarating. She saw Missy running for the hoop, she tossed her a quick pass and Missy scored two points with a lay-up. The walls of the gym were shaking from the roar of the crowd.

There was no time to enjoy it, however, the game kept going. The Tartans lined up into their man-to-man full-court press. Elena and Missy forced the Buffaloes to turn over the ball to them at half court and called a time out.

The noise was immense, the band was playing the school song and the fans were singing along as the five players ran over to the bench.

"Good play, Paivi, but don't leave Brooke West by herself again. That's dangerous. Now, go out there and run the play for Leyla, keep up the momentum!" Coach Espinosa screamed, her voice lost in the noise of the crowd.

The girls lined up at half court and were able to get the ball in quickly and set up their offense. They set their picks and moved around the court. Leyla fought hard to get open.

"Run it again!" Leyla shouted at Missy, and the girls went through the play again.

Two Buffaloes double-teamed Leyla under the basket. Paivi was left alone, wide open, on the opposite side. Elena, with the ball at the top of the key, saw Paivi and dished her a pass. Paivi went up for a lay-up and scored. As she was coming down from the shot, a Buffalo took her legs out from under her, sending her crashing to the floor.

Foul. One shot.

Paivi's teammates helped her up and she headed to the free-throw line. It was hard to focus; she could barely hear herself think. She stood at the line and took a deep breath. The referee took a look around and gave Paivi the ball. She looked at the basket, lined herself up, bent her knees and felt her body go through the motions. She released the ball and watched it as it silently spun through the air. It felt like time had stopped.

SWISH

The ball sailed straight through the hoop, without even touching the rim. Paivi breathed after what seemed like an eternity. The crowd went wild. The score was now 70-65. Only one minute left. The Buffaloes were frantic. They attempted to get off another shot during the last minute to no avail. The Tartans played out the last few seconds, passing the ball around the court to run out the clock.

At the buzzer, scores of cheering fans ran out onto the floor to congratulate the Tartans. The team gathered at center court to receive the tournament trophy.

Paivi hung back a little, looking around the crowd for her parents and for Jason. She spotted Christian in the midst of the crowd. He met her eye and smiled. She scowled and turned away.

They hadn't won because she played hard. They'd won because she had cheated. She was angry, angry with herself for using the tip and that she was letting Christian win. Now he had even more dirt on her. And he knew she could be used just like he used everyone else.

She turned back to the team.

Maybe it wasn't so bad, she thought, looking at how happy they all were. *I did it for them, for our team. I didn't do it just for me.*

The girls were passing the trophy around to have their pictures taken. Paivi posed for a few and then headed over to the bench to pick up her things. As she approached the bench, she could see Coach Espinosa surrounded by the local reporters. The three reporters turned to Paivi with their notepads and tape recorders.

"Paivi, great game!" said the first reporter, a short, stocky man with a moustache and a baseball hat. "I'm Dan

Reinhard from the St. Andrew Herald. What were you thinking during the overtime? That steal was spectacular! It changed the whole tide of the game!"

"Well, I, uh, I don't know. I was just doing what I could to help the team, you know," she stammered, a little surprised by the sudden attention.

"You know, you held All-Stater Brooke West to just eight points. That was some amazing defense. Her average is around twenty-five points, you know. How did you do it?" asked a tall, skinny man.

"Well, Coach Espinosa told me not to let her score, so I just did the best I could," she answered, happy to turn the conversation to something she had accomplished without Christian Nelson. "And the other girls helped me by doubling down any time Brooke had the ball."

"Steve Johnstone." The third man stuck his hand out. Paivi shook it. "Tartan Times. You must have felt really good about that shot in the overtime. Your points put the game to bed."

"I guess, but it was only three points out of seventy," said Paivi. "It's like, nothing."

"Well, thanks for your time, Paivi. You are truly a team player," said the second reporter. He snapped his notebook closed and moved to talk to the Buffaloes coach. The other two reporters nodded and followed him across the floor.

There was still a large crowd in the gym after Paivi's team meeting had ended. She spotted her parents and Torsten first and went up to greet them.

"Great game Sweetheart!" said Mr. Anderson, giving her a big hug. "I'm so proud of you! You really gave the old ticker a run for its money. What a steal and what a basket. All I can say is wow!"

"Thanks, Dad." She tried to lighten up a little bit. She didn't want her parents to think anything was wrong. This was something she would have to keep to herself. Well, to herself and one other person.

"Why don't we go out for ice cream to celebrate?" asked an excited Mrs. Anderson, patting Paivi on the shoulder.

"Can I invite Aimee?" Torsten glanced sideways at Paivi.

She said nothing. Torsten was the least of her problems.

"Of course, Tor, that's fine. She can ride with us if she likes. Just make sure she calls her parents," Mrs. Anderson called after Tor, who had already sprinted off in Aimee's general direction.

"Paivi, I just saw the Lorenzos, and I want to say hi to them, so go visit with your friends and see if anyone is up for ice cream. We'll leave in ten minutes." Mrs. Anderson tapped her watch.

Mr. and Mrs. Anderson wandered off towards a large group of adults near the door.

Paivi could hear Michaela's loud voice in the crowd and started to follow it. She greeted a few people she knew from around school and headed into the throng of students. Out of nowhere she felt someone grab her from the side and arms slid around her waist. She was lifted the air and spun around in a circle.

"You were amazing!" shouted a familiar voice.

She smiled. Jason.

He set her back on the floor, spinning her around to face him.

"Dude—that was an amazing game! The steal was just unbelievable and man, you gave that big girl a run for her money!" he said excitedly.

He pulled her close and she threw her arms around his neck, hugging him. She pulled back quickly, remembering that her jersey was soaked with sweat and hoping she didn't stink too badly.

"Come on." Paivi grabbed Jason's hand. He squeezed hers back and didn't pull away. "I have to find Michaela."

He followed her as they wove through the crowd. Paivi continued to follow the sound of Michaela's voice.

"OHMYGODPAIVI!" squealed Michaela as she launched herself off the bleachers and on to Paivi. "That was amazing! You're a beast!"

"Do either of you want to come with us for ice cream?" Paivi said, glancing nervously at Jason. She wasn't comfortable asking Jason to go out unless other friends were involved. She was pretty sure he liked her; after all, he did ask her out for Saturday and he was still holding her hand. She hoped that their little date would help them figure out if they were more than friends or not. She was definitely hoping so.

"Yeah, sure," answered Jason quickly.

"Dude, like I would turn down ice cream! Lead the way!" Michaela laughed.

"Come on, let's go find my mom." Paivi grabbed Michaela's arm and dragged her along. As they turned around, she came face to face with Christian Nelson and some members of his usual entourage.

She didn't know what to say.

"Paivi that was an awesome game! I mean, that steal, wow!" he paused, giving her a knowing look.

"Uh, yeah, it was pretty crazy." She hardened her gaze a bit, hoping he could read that she wasn't pleased.

"So, how about that Chicago and Green Bay game this Sunday? It looks like a good one too. Are you going to watch it?" Christian asked, smirking. She looked away. Sometimes she just wanted to smash him in the face, if only that were socially acceptable. He was just so smug.

"It's cool," he responded, picking up on her discomfort. "I'll give you a call tomorrow. Have a good night, Paivi! Sweet dreams!"

He waved and chuckled as his group sauntered away.

A wave of nausea washed over her. She still had to figure out that score tonight. If she didn't, well she didn't want to think about what he would do.

"Are you friends with that guy?" asked Jason, eyeing Christian suspiciously.

"Well, I wouldn't call him a friend." She thought for a minute. "But he's alright. He's harmless."

She just hoped that was true.

Chapter Twelve

Visions

Paivi was able to relax at Lolly's Ice Cream Shoppe. It all just felt so comfortable. Jason and Mr. Anderson were discussing baseball over their hot fudge sundaes. Paivi and Michaela were reminiscing about things that Torsten had done when he was younger. Mrs. Anderson and Aimee were laughing along with the girls. Torsten could only shake his head in embarrassment, and sink lower into his seat.

"And remember," howled Michaela, "when we were at Taco Caliente that one time? We were waiting for our food and Torsten was gone. All of a sudden we heard this mooing sound. We turned around and there was Torsten, hiding in the plants next to the counter, mooing like a cow!"

She pretended like she was separating some invisible plants and stuck her head through.

"MOOOO!"

Paivi was laughing so hard she started choking on her hot fudge brownie sundae. After she was able to swallow again, the girls collapsed into laughter. They were laughing so hard that they were crying, tears streaming down their faces.

"Dude, I was like nine years old," protested Torsten meekly.

They returned home around eleven, after dropping everyone off at their homes. Paivi said goodnight to her parents and Torsten and headed up to her room. She had to pretend she was going to bed, but she felt it would be a long time before she got any sleep.

She shut her door and lit a candle, placing it on her desk. She turned out the light and could hear everyone else in settling into their rooms for the night. She sat on her bed, folded her long legs Indian-style and rested her hands on her knees. She remembered seeing people meditate this way in a movie.

She took a few deep breaths, focusing her gaze on the candle.

Score of the Chicago-Green Bay game, she chanted over and over in her mind. She tried to picture people playing football, and even Soldier Field itself, which she'd only ever seen on television. After about twenty minutes of watching the candlelight dance on the wall and peeking at the glowing numbers on her alarm clock, she gave up. Paivi blew out the candle in a huff and angrily got into bed, stuffed animals flying right and left.

What was she going to do? Maybe she'd have to break down and talk to her parents. Maybe they knew how to control this and just kept it from her, or maybe they could get the score for her.

What was she thinking, though? If she told her parents, they would know Christian was blackmailing her.

What would they do? March into school and talk to the principal? Worse yet, what would Christian do?

It was all too much. She grabbed Mr. Teddy Bear off the floor where she had thrown him, squeezing him tight. A few hot, angry tears rolled down her cheek, wetting her pillow.

When she opened her eyes, she was sitting in her family room. The television was on, showing the last play of a football game between the Chicago Bears and the Green Bay Packers. Mr. Anderson was sitting on the edge of the couch and Torsten was on his knees in front of the screen. Both teams were at the line of scrimmage with two minutes left on the clock. Green Bay had the ball and the score was tied.

"How are they going to win this game?" shouted Paivi. "Tor, move your big fat head. I can't see."

She threw a pillow at him.

"They HAVE to win!" screamed Torsten. "We can't lose to those idiots!"

"Shhhhhh!" Mr. Anderson's gaze was glued to the screen as he hushed them.

Green Bay ran the ball down the field, picking up a few yards. On the next play, the Green Bay quarterback threw the ball and it sailed through the air towards a player in green and white. Out of nowhere a member of the Bears jumped into the picture. He snatched the ball out of the air, right in front of the ball's intended target and sprinted down to the opposite end of the field.

"Go, go, go!" they all screamed.

Into the Shadows

Mr. Anderson jumped off the couch, knocking a bowl off the table, sending popcorn cascading across the floor.

Chicago's number 23 wove in and out of the players on the field, zigging and zagging. He ran into the end zone and the referees signaled a touchdown.

"Yeah!" they all screamed, Paivi and Torsten jumped up and down, exchanging high-fives.

"Yahoo!" shouted Mr. Anderson, throwing his blue and orange Bears cap in the air.

An extra point was kicked, leading to more cheering as the clock ran out. Paivi looked at the screen, noticing the score of 21-14.

Paivi sat back down on the couch and closed her eyes.

When she opened them again, her family room was gone. She could feel the ground below her feet. She looked around, completely unfamiliar with her surroundings. The ground was hard and dusty; there was no grass to be seen. In the distance, she could see high, rocky peaks. In front of her was row after row of large, metal buildings, the same dusty brown color as the ground.

The sun was high in the sky, the air hot. There was not a soul to be seen. Paivi heard the sound of an engine in the distance. Someone was coming. She didn't think she should be there. Everything felt wrong. She panicked and tried to move from where she was, looking for a place to hide. Her feet wouldn't budge—they were glued to the spot.

Oh god, please don't let them see me, she thought,

her heart beginning to race.

To the right was a large metal fence, topped with razor wire that glinted like diamonds in the hot sun. Paivi could see four trucks in the distance. Two trucks led what appeared to be a large group people, and two followed behind. As they got closer, Paivi could see that there were men in the back of each truck, wearing some kind of uniform. They pointed large guns at the group.

The trucks entered through a gate, which moved aside as the truck approached. They drove right past Paivi, taking no notice of her. The men wore sand colored clothing and floppy hats, which shielded their heads and faces from the blistering sun. Behind the two trucks came the column of people. Paivi had to look closely to see that they were all women. It was hard to tell at first. She couldn't decide if their clothes were meant to be brown or were so on account of all the dust.

The women were very thin and most were either browned or reddened from the harsh sun. They looked like so many bundles of rags held up by sticks. None of the women turned to look at Paivi, but she could see that while all of their faces were different, they were all frighteningly the same. The eyes were dull and sunken—their lips were dried and shriveled, like plants that hadn't been watered in ages. These women had given up hope long ago.

As they passed by Paivi, moving mechanically like so many zombies, a woman turned, staring directly at her. Her empty eyes burned into Paivi, and she could feel a scream stuck in her throat. She knew this sunken miserable shell of a person.

It was her mother.

Paivi woke in a tangle of blankets, soaked in sweat and gasping for air. She jumped out of bed and lunged for the light switch. The room was instantly bathed in light. Paivi looked around wildly, not knowing what to do. She sat down on the bed, shaking her head. What did this mean? Clearly, something horrible was going to happen. But when? And why? She rubbed her face with her hands. She wanted to run in and wake her parents up. She wanted to tell them everything she had seen. But what good would that do? She had no answers.

Hey, Mom and Dad, I saw Mom in my dream and she was in some camp near some mountains. She looked half dead.

She pictured the conversation and it just seemed ridiculous.

Remembering the score of the football game that she would need to give Christian in the morning, she grabbed a pen and jotted down 21-14 Chicago on a notepad.

She turned off the light and returned to bed. The alarm clock numbers glowed in the darkness. She lay there, watching them slowly change until she fell into a restless sleep.

The next morning, she opened her eyes slowly, feeling like she hadn't slept at all. She saw herself in the bathroom mirror and made a face. She touched the huge dark circles under her eyes. Thankfully, Coach Espinosa had given them the day off after their big win the night before. She didn't feel up to practice today.

Last night seemed like years away now. She went down to breakfast. It was late, past ten, and Mr. and Mrs. Anderson had already left to do some shopping.

'*Good Morning Sunshine!*' read a sticky note attached to a pile of newspapers. '*Hope you got some rest! Enjoy the papers! Love, Mom and Dad.*'

Torsten came stumbling down the stairs, rubbing his eyes as Paivi looked through the stack of papers. The St. Andrew Herald, the Tartan Times, and the Tribune all had her picture on the front page, stealing the ball from number 15. The headline above read 'Tartans Take Tournament.' The caption under her picture read 'St. Andrew High School's center, Paivi Anderson, saves the day. See Sports for the full report.'

"Mom and Dad gone already?" mumbled Torsten through a yawn.

"Yeah," she answered, shuffling through the papers, looking for the Sports sections. The back page had the headline 'Anderson stops West: Leads SAHS to Victory' above a picture of her guarding Brooke West.

She couldn't even muster enough energy to get excited about seeing her name in the paper. She had cheated. And after her dream, she didn't really care much about any of it any more. What did it matter if she did well in a basketball game when she had seen her mother in some horrible camp, looking half dead? She pushed the papers aside and headed to the pantry. She grabbed her favorite cereal, Fruity Puffs, along with a bowl and a spoon, setting it all on the table. She dumped out a heap of cereal and grabbed some milk from the fridge to add to it. She pulled the comics page out from the pile of papers and began to read them as she ate her breakfast.

"What, don't you want to read all the glorious articles about the wonder and magnificent Paivi Anderson?"

"No," she answered curtly, hoping he would take a hint.

"Well, I don't know about you," Torsten pulled out a chair across from Paivi, sitting down with a giant stack of microwave pancakes and two jars, one of peanut butter and one of jelly, "but I would love to have someone put my picture all over the papers."

Paivi said nothing and shoveled another spoonful of Fruity Puffs into her mouth. How could he even begin to understand this?

"What, now you're too good to talk to me?" Torsten struggled to get the words around a mouthful of peanut butter and jelly pancakes.

"Look, just leave me alone." She glared at him across the table. He shrank at the sharpness of her voice. He snatched the sports section from the pile and put it up so Paivi couldn't see his face.

They spent the rest of breakfast in silence. After she finished eating, she called Christian's house. The answering machine picked up, so she left a message. She called Jason and told him she was sick and couldn't make it to a movie. He did sound extremely disappointed and promised to take her another time when she was feeling better. Not feeling like doing much else, she went back up to her room. She wanted to be alone. Her bed looked so warm and inviting. She was so tired and wanted to try to make herself see more of the images of her mother at the camp to try and figure out how she got there, but she just couldn't muster the energy.

Paivi crawled back under her covers and closed her eyes.

No more dreams, she told herself, as she drifted off into a deep sleep.

Chapter Thirteen

Infamy

Paivi Anderson
Current Events p.6
Dr. Hasenpfeffer

In the <u>St. Andrew Herald</u> article 'Nation anxious for action', by Jerome Knowles, he interviews people in and around St. Andrew to see what they are hoping the Anti-Terrorism Coalition will achieve. Everyone is looking forward to a meeting on Sunday, when the ATC will announce their plan for stopping the terrorists. The ATC has already recruited thousands of new officers, helping the poor economy by getting the unemployed young people off the streets and back to work. Knowles found that the community appreciates the opportunities that the ATC offers those who have gone so long without work. Also, he reports that most people are positive that the ATC will make a major impact on the war on terrorism. I agree and feel that it is important that we support the government in hopes that they can make this country safer.

Interesting article. A

President-Elect Wendell Stevens filed into the Capitol Building's rotunda with the other members of the newly formed Anti-Terrorism Coalition. Together they represented the major offices of the government. Trailing behind him down the hall were Celine Mattucci from the State Department, General Michael Kobayashi of the U.S. Army, Daniel Foster, director of the FBI and Deshaun Haley, head of the CIA.

A raised platform was set up on one side of the rotunda, along with a large table with five chairs. The audience was filled with reporters and rows of cameramen from the many different news stations. The members of the Anti-Terrorism Coalition made their way to their seats. President-Elect Stevens took the center chair. He could see the Secret Service agents stationed all around the room.

"We're ready when you are," said a man in front of the platform, wearing a headset and carrying a clipboard.

Senator Stevens looked into the camera and began to speak into the microphone.

"My fellow Americans, thank you for joining us this evening. We, as a country, have suffered deeply from the constant attacks of the Righteous Front, or RF. As you may recall, I had received some information, which would be able to aid our nation in ending the terrorist threat that exists in every town across this great nation. As I promised, we created the Anti-Terrorism Coalition to administer the great task that stands before us. Together with the different governmental agencies, the Armed Forces, the FBI, the CIA, and the State Department, we have been able to prepare a program that will ensure the safety of all Americans. The information I received was a long list of possible traitors with whom we would like to meet and interview. As it has been reported, we have already identified some criminals that we have in custody who have ties to the RF. To explain the process, here is Ms. Celine Mattucci of the State Department."

"Thank you, Senator." She nodded in his direction. "In tomorrow's newspapers, in every city and town across the United States, there will be a list of people in the local area that we would like to interview. We expect anyone whose name appears on this list to report to the location listed in the newspaper by five tomorrow evening. You will be assisted by local members of the Anti-Terrorism Coalition. If you in any way attempt to deviate from this process, you will be considered a traitor to this country and you will be promptly arrested and all of your rights will be forfeited. This also pertains to any newspapers refusing to print the lists as they have been ordered. Any found not in compliance will be shut down and all employees will need to register with the ATC as well. ATC agents will also be present in communities across the country to assist local law enforcement with this massive undertaking. This process is meant to be quick and efficient. We are hoping that all citizens posted on this list will understand that this process is for the good of all Americans. We all want to live in a safe country with no fear of terrorist attacks. With your cooperation, we hope to make that possible. Thank you and good night."

The end of the address caused the reporters to explode in a barrage of questions.

"Is this process legal?"

"This doesn't sound supported by the Constitution. What do you have to say in defense of that, President-Elect Stevens?"

He stood up and took the microphone.

"Ladies and gentleman, I understand your concerns," he had a large grin on his face, "but I assure you that this certainly is legal under the Constitution of these United States. This group is absolutely committed to following a proper legal process. Our intentions are completely pure here. We are just looking to protect our citizens—to save mothers and fathers, sons and daughters from the evils of terrorism and nothing more. We thank you for your time. We will not be taking any more questions this evening."

The questions swirled around them as they stepped down from the platform, flanked by men in dark suits, and were led down a corridor away from the crowd of reporters.

They entered a conference room and took seats around the table, sitting stiffly in the large, cumbersome chairs.

"I think that went well." President-Elect Stevens poured himself a glass of bourbon from a decanter in the middle of the table. "It appears that Phase One is ready to roll. I don't anticipate many problems. Kobayashi, where are we on Phase Two?"

"Phase Two is currently at fifty percent completion.

It is scheduled to be ready by your inauguration."

"Foster, Haley, you have your procedures in place for Phase Two?"

"Yes, sir," answered Deshaun Haley. "We have task forces from our groups running simulations. Efficiency is key here."

"Couldn't have said it better myself!" President-Elect Stevens swirled the bourbon in his glass.

"Everything needs to run quickly and quietly as well. The parcels need to be moved to the facility within a week of inauguration. Earlier, if possible. They have to be processed and out of the general population before they know what hit them. Then the ATC can commence with Phase Three," added Haley.

"I'm so impressed. You have thought of everything. I like what I hear. And I promise you, if we can make it from Phase One to Phase Three without a hitch, you will all be rewarded. You are the ones who truly understand the importance of this operation. The safety of this nation depends on it. If we can put an end to these terrorists, this will go down as the most influential administration since Abraham Lincoln." He leaned back in the large chair and folded his hands contentedly over his expansive belly.

Paivi spent the rest of the weekend in a fog. When she wasn't sleeping, she was attempting to force her mind back into the visions of her mother at the camp with no success. She spent the rest of the time laying on the couch in the family room, frustrated and tired.

Christian had finally called her back on Sunday morning. The conversation was brief. She wasn't in the mood for chatting.

"21-14 Chicago," she mumbled into the phone.

"Nice job, Paivi. I knew I could count on you! I gotta go—I have some calls to make. See you at school tomorrow."

"Okay, bye." She feebly let the phone drop from her ear. She didn't care about Christian and his stupid game. She didn't even care about him exposing her family anymore. What did it matter anyways? She saw what was going to happen. The fact that Christian could be the one to cause that horrible vision continued to haunt her. Paivi couldn't forget her mother's eyes. But she couldn't figure out how it was possible for Christian to cause her mother to end up in a place like that. She doubted he had access to his own prison camp.

And what was this place? she kept asking herself.

She remembered the dusty ground and the rocky peaks that surrounded the cage-like enclosure. It looked like it could be somewhere out west, maybe in Nevada or Arizona, she guessed. The Andersons had traveled to the Grand Canyon and Las Vegas a few years back, and the landscape looked similar.

Thinking about it only made her feel worse, and she knew she had to get herself together. No one would understand and she didn't want people asking questions. Her parents had showed some concern already, asking if she was feeling all right. She told them she wasn't feeling well, which really wasn't a lie.

Paivi woke up Monday morning feeling a little better. School would be a nice distraction to help her get the awful images out of her head. After a quick shower, she threw on jeans and a t-shirt and headed downstairs to grab some breakfast. She walked into the kitchen to find her parents talking quietly over the newspaper. Her mother looked like she had been crying.

"John, I just don't understand! We're good people! Why on earth are our names on this horrible list? We aren't terrorists!"

"Honey, I know. I don't know what's going on any more than you do."

The floor squeaked as Paivi stepped into the doorway. Her parents jumped and exchanged a desperate glance.

"Paivi...um...you and your brother will have to stay home from school today. And I suppose we aren't going to work either." He picked up the newspaper and slid it across the table to Paivi. "We are on the Anti-Terrorism Coalition's list. We have to go to their office at city hall today by five or we could be in some trouble."

"Dad, I don't understand." Paivi felt a bit sick.

"Neither do we honey, neither do we." He put his arm around Mrs. Anderson as he sat down at the table.

Paivi joined them at the table, not taking her eyes off of the newspaper. There had to be a few hundred people on the list. She recognized some of them, Officer Brickman, who worked with Mr. Anderson, Christian Nelson and his parents, Elena Pappas from her basketball team and Mr. Kingsley, a science teacher at St. Andrew High. The list had their names, addresses, birthdates, and employers or schools. There was no way to hide with all of that information revealed. She was surprised they didn't have pictures posted as well.

"So they must know about us, about what we can do," observed Paivi.

"That's what we thought," sniffled Mrs. Anderson. "But how could they know?"

"I don't know, but I do know one of the boys on the list, Christian Nelson. He goes to my school. And I know he's like us," Paivi admitted. "But there are so many people on that list. Can they all do something special?"

"We recognized most of the people on the list that are like us. They are all good people. Where would they get the idea that we're terrorists?" She spat the word out like it was poison.

Torsten burst into the room at that moment, still in his pajamas.

"Mom, can I have...," he trailed off, taking in the atmosphere of the room. "Uh, who died?"

Paivi handed her brother the newspaper.

"I don't understand," he started, as his eyes scanned the list.

"Join the club," Paivi interrupted.

"But this is stupid! We're not terrorists!" His eyes flashed.

She could see Torsten was truly angry, which didn't

happen often.

"You're both just going to have to stay home today so we can go and figure this out," offered Mr. Anderson.

They decided to head to City Hall early, to get the process over with. As they got into the SUV, Mr. Anderson tried to remain positive. "We'll just head down there and get this all straightened out. There has obviously been some kind of misunderstanding." He backed the SUV down the driveway.

A lump rose in Paivi's throat. There had to be another way.

"Mommy, Daddy, please, I saw something, and I think it might have to do with this list stuff. I saw Mom in a dream and she was in some kind of camp and she looked awful." She continued rambling, pleading, not wanting to stop. "Look, maybe we should just keep driving. Can't we just drive to Canada or something? We're only like four hours away!"

Torsten stared at her.

"Honey, we've discussed this. We've seen a few things too. But we can't leave. This is our life here. And if we leave now, everyone will think we are the bad guys or helping them. We owe it to ourselves to stay and prove that we are innocent. We are good people and we can hope that our friends and family see the truth. We are not running," answered Mr. Anderson firmly, his eyes on hers in the review mirror.

Paivi leaned sulkily against the window, as they passed the neatly groomed lawns in the tidy St. Andrew neighborhoods. The gray sky and light drizzle added a misty haze to the already dreary day. A sense of dread coursed through her, running up and down her body before settling in her stomach. The neat little houses looked strangely alien to her now, not as warm and cozy as they used to appear.

After parking the car, the Andersons walked slowly across the St. Andrew City Hall parking lot, avoiding the large puddles that had collected from days of rain. Mrs. Anderson held Mr. Anderson's arm tightly. Paivi and Torsten trudged silently behind.

City Hall was a very uninteresting building made of metal and glass. Unlike many of the historic buildings in St. Andrew, it was built in the late nineteen-sixties and instead of charming it just looked a bit boring and tired. They entered the lobby and joined a line of people in the nondescript hallway. The carpet was worn and stained in spots, and the walls painted white, which made the fluorescent lights glow brighter. Paivi observed the people in line, their faces pale and solemn. Despite the crowd, the hallway was very quiet. She could hear a few small children whining to their parents about being tired and wanting to sit down.

The line moved slowly towards a set of double doors at the end of the hallway. Paivi didn't notice anyone coming out of the office, but she did notice the two armed guards on either side of the doors. They were dressed in black from head to toe, the only exception was a glowing silver badge they each wore on their breast pocket. The white letters read ATC. They also wore armbands on their right arms bearing the same letters, but these were not nearly as impressive as the glowing badges. On their heads were black caps, similar to a policeman's cap, which bore a silver eagle just above the brim.

Paivi's eyes were not so much drawn to these aspects of the men's appearances—instead they were glued to the large machine guns that the men carried in their arms. The only gun she had ever seen in real life was her father's service revolver, given to him by the St. Andrew Police Department. The gun barrels were pointed towards the doorway, so that as each person passed, it was pointed at their heads. Both men were expressionless, looking straight ahead— giant, menacing statues.

Paivi shifted nervously from one foot to another. She hoped once they registered, they could just go home and have a normal day tomorrow, like none of this had happened.

Finally, it was their turn to go through the door. Paivi did not like the sensation of guns being pointed at her head, even if the people holding them didn't appear to intend to use them. Paivi and Torsten followed their parents closely, not wanting to be the first ones to reach their destination. They were led through a room by a woman, dressed in black like the men at the door and wearing the same glowing badge and armband they had sported. She walked them to a desk where they took a seat in some stiff, metal folding chairs in front of a man wearing the now familiar ATC uniform.

He looked up as they sat down, an indifferent expression in his eyes.

"Name?" he demanded.

Mr. Anderson was a bit flustered by the man's abruptness.

"I, uh, I'm John Anderson. This is my wife, Maria and my children, Paivi and Torsten."

The man entered some information on the computer in front of him. He then handed Mr. Anderson a booklet.

"This contains all of the information that you'll need. You are all considered to be possible Enemies of the State, so you are currently being placed under what we call work-home-containment. You are allowed to be away from your home between the hours of 5 A.M. and 5 P.M., only for work purposes. Children are also required to be home by the 5 P.M. curfew. Weekend curfews are also in place. Adults will remain in the home with the exception of the hours from 7 to 8 A.M. on Saturdays when they are allowed to go to the grocery store in town. Children are allowed out of the home from 9 A.M. until 9 P.M. on the weekend."

Another man in an ATC uniform dropped off a box to the man at the desk and waited for him to look at the writing on it and nod. He then scurried off.

"Also, due to the fact that you are considered dangerous, you, as possible Enemies of the State, referred to hereafter as EOS, will have your passports revoked. This means that it will not be possible for you to leave this country or enter any other country."

Paivi took a quick glance at her parents. Their eyes were wide and their skin had taken on a sickly pallor. She looked back to the man at the desk, fearing if she looked at them again, she'd burst into tears.

"Note that information has been sent to your schools and employers, and certain policies will be in place starting tomorrow to help them better deal with your situation. Lastly, here are your EOS badges. Each of you has been issued an EOS badge with a number, which will identify you to the ATC officers in the area." He opened the box, which displayed four round, silver badges. They were attached to a charger and glowed like the ones the ATC officers were wearing. However, they glowed with a deep red light. Each badge had the capital letters EOS and two initials underneath, which Paivi assumed represented their first and last names. On the same line as the initials stood a number, each one different. The man took the badges from the box and handed one to each of the Andersons.

"By law, you are required to wear your EOS badge at all times when you are outside of your home. When you are at home, your badges must be placed back in the charger. If they are not all back in the charger by curfew, ATC responders will be immediately dispatched to arrest you."

"Mr, um, Mr…?" Mr. Anderson paused, waiting for the ATC officer to give his name. He didn't. "Okay, sir," he continued. "I am a police officer in this town. I know my rights. This infringes on every right given to me by our Constitution. I demand an explanation!"

His voice had risen, causing ATC officers at the other desks around the room to glance over in alarm. A few ATC officers began to move in their direction. Paivi sank down into her seat as far as she could, trying to avoid the stares.

The ATC officer in front of them raised his hand, indicating to his fellow officers that he had the situation under control.

"Mr. Anderson, in your situation, it is not advisable to make a scene," he leaned back in his chair. "According to the government of the United States of America, those rights no longer apply to you or your family. I have explained your new rights to you. If you know what's good for you, you will quietly take your family home," he stood up, as if to signify their meeting had ended. "And I should also mention that you will be subject to private interviews with the ATC. They will contact you."

Mr. and Mrs. Anderson rose from their seats, as did Paivi and Torsten. Her parents looked like balloons that had lost their air, their shoulders sagging and faces drooping. They put their arms around Paivi and Torsten, holding them close.

"Don't forget to put your EOS badges on," the ATC officer gestured to the exit.

The Andersons moved towards the back door in a daze. The ride home was silent. The only sound was that of Mrs. Anderson crying softly in the front seat. Paivi looked at the badge affixed to her coat. The silver looked dull in the gray light of the day. The letters stood out, slightly warm to the touch. Under the letters EOS stood her initials: PA. Next to that were six numbers: 150778.

She looked across the car at Torsten. He was also inspecting his badge. He looked up, noticing she was watching, and stopped, turning instead to look out of the window. She leaned back in her seat and returned to looking at the homes as they passed back through St. Andrew towards home. She couldn't believe she would have to wear this stupid thing to school. She thought about what her friends would say, who else would have one, and what would Jason think. She had hoped this would all just go away, the dreams, Christian, everything. But instead, she would be wearing it right on her shirt for all to see.

    She thought back to what the man had said about the curfew. She hoped maybe they would adjust the times for her basketball games; after all, she was not the only one with a curfew problem on the team. Elena Pappas was one of their best players and she couldn't imagine the team would want to play without them. Or would they? She leaned her head against the window; the dread was traveling again, spreading and extinguishing hope. Tomorrow was going to be the first day of school all over again. Only this time, she would be the one wearing a glowing badge, advertising her as a big, fat freak.

Chapter Fourteen

Policies

Paivi carefully packed her gym bag for basketball practice that crisp, sunny Tuesday morning. She looked her outfit over in the mirror, carefully affixing her new silver badge with the red glowing letters and numbers to her purple hoodie. She studied her reflection carefully.

It's not so bad, she thought. Maybe people won't even notice.

She tossed her long, blond hair over her shoulder. She could still see the red light glowing through the strands, but it was much less noticeable. Paivi headed downstairs for a piece of toast, though she didn't feel very hungry.

Mrs. Anderson was going to drive both Paivi and Torsten to school. Mr. and Mrs. Anderson felt it was best for them to avoid the school bus, at least until they were comfortable with their new accessories. Paivi and Torsten didn't argue.

Paivi was slightly nervous—she hadn't spoken to any of her friends since the list was released. She kept reminding herself that she had been friends with many of them since grade school. One stupid, silver, glowing button couldn't ruin what she'd had with her friends for seven years.

The ride to school was quiet. When her mother reached the school parking lot, Paivi sighed in relief. Everything here looked comfortably the same. Students parked their cars and others were getting off of busses—the usual noise and chaos of a regular morning before school.

Paivi got out of the car; carefully making sure her hair had fallen over the glowing pin. She headed towards the front entrance of the school, spotting Michaela, Aimee, and Crystal near the steps and headed over to join them.

"Hey guys!" she tried to sound as upbeat and normal as usual.

"Paivi!" squealed Michaela, throwing her arms around Paivi. "I missed you yesterday and I didn't get to talk to you all weekend! It feels like years! Where were you?"

Paivi didn't feel like going into all the details.

"My parents made me stay home. It was pretty lame," she answered.

"We thought maybe it was because you were on that list in the paper," Michaela spoke a little more quietly. She looked concerned. "My dad told me about it, but we just couldn't figure out why you, your parents, Elena, Christian, and all those other people were on the list. What did your parents say?"

Aimee and Crystal were watching the conversation with interest, like spectators at a tennis match.

"They were pretty upset. I mean, we're on this list and they won't even tell us why. None of us have ever broken the law, let alone helped terrorists. It's all just crazy! It's got to be some kind of misunderstanding," Paivi said, her voice low. "Yesterday we had to go to City Hall, and they gave us a bunch of rules to follow, like we have a curfew and we have to wear these stupid pins." She brushed her hair back, exposing the silver badge. "Anyways, we have to do this until they interview us. Hopefully that will be soon, so everything can just go back to normal."

Michaela fingered the silver badge.

"Well, it is ugly isn't it? Maybe I could glue some sequins to it to give it a little pizzazz!"

"Very funny," chuckled Paivi, feeling happy that she had been right about her friends. "Come on, let's go inside. I'm freezing!"

As the girls entered through the main doors into the cafeteria, Paivi noticed something out of the ordinary. Four men, dressed all in black with the now all too familiar ATC badges glowing on their shirts, stood with arms folded across their chests. They had positioned themselves so that the students had to go around them. Paivi's heart began to thump so loudly in her chest that she worried they would hear it. One of the agents spotted her right away.

"You." He pointed right at Paivi, eyeing her badge.

The students all around them stared at her, more frightened of the agents than of her, at least.

"Go over there." The agent pointed to the side of the cafeteria.

Stunned, she shuffled to the side of the stream of students, unable to utter even a goodbye to her friends. At one of the lunch tables sat about a dozen other extremely miserable looking students, slouching down as far as they could. Some had even put their heads down on the table, hiding their faces in folded arms. She spotted Christian's white-blond hair and headed over to sit by him. She said nothing as she slid onto the stool opposite him. He looked up, eyes ringed with dark circles, but otherwise looking as cocky as ever.

"So I guess a 'good' morning isn't really in order," he offered.

"Yeah, not so much."

"Paivi." His eyes were serious. "It's gonna be a bad day."

"Way to cheer me up." She smiled sarcastically.

He nodded in the direction of the agents.

"I know they're here to give us more rules." He glanced at her gym bag. "No more basketball for you."

Her jaw dropped. "What? No way. They can't do that!"

"Paivi," he whispered, "they took away all of our constitutional freedoms in one day and you're surprised that they are going to kick you off the basketball team? Come on!"

"Well, I just don't see what our activities have to do with all of this. They'll figure something out," she insisted.

"Whatever." He rolled his eyes at her. "I wouldn't lie to you about that."

"I...I know," she answered quietly, fiddling with the zipper on her gym bag.

The warning bell for first hour rang and the crowd moving through the cafeteria had almost completely thinned out. Three of the four ATC agents came over to their table. Paivi noticed each of them had a holster containing a handgun, not unlike the one her dad carried at work.

"Good morning students," began the agent standing in the middle. "We will now be escorting you to room thirteen, where we will meet with the principal to detail the policies you will have here at school."

The bell rang, and the fourth agent joined them. Without saying a word, the students rose to follow the agents, who broke into two pairs, flanking the group in the front and behind to ensure none of them deviated from their route. Paivi was grateful that everyone was in class with the doors closed. She didn't want to be seen being herded down the hallway by men with guns.

They entered room thirteen and took seats in some empty desks lined up in rows. The principal, Mr. Carson, and the assistant principal, Ms. Merriweather, stood waiting at the front of the room. Their faces were tense, mouths set into a firm line.

"I would like to address my students before you begin," requested Mr. Carson, speaking to the man who appeared to be the leader of the ATC agents. He nodded his head.

"Kids, I just want to say that we value you. The school did not create the new rules that the ATC has mandated. Please come and see us if you have any problems. Thank you."

"What are you implying, Principal Carson?" demanded the now red-faced ATC agent.

"I'm not trying to imply anything. I am just factually informing the students from whence the rules came. They are a creation of the ATC, are they not?"

"That is correct," stated the agent, looking like he wanted to add a few more things to his response, but decided against it.

Mr. Carson stepped back, gesturing to the ATC agent to take the floor. He and Ms. Merriweather looked on sternly, arms crossed.

"It is a privilege for you to still be able to attend school. I am here to inform you of the policies that the ATC has developed for EOS students. My name is Agent O'Higgins. We will be stationed here at St. Andrew High School. If any of these rules are broken, you will be immediately expelled from school and subject to house arrest."

As Agent O'Higgins spoke, one of the other agents handed each student a booklet.

"Inside this booklet you will find the information that I will explain to you today. First, you must all wear your EOS badges at all times, which has already been explained to you at your local ATC office. Your lockers have now been moved to a designated EOS area, directly in front of the main office. In each class, EOS students need to sit at the special table at the front of the room, next to the teacher. In the cafeteria, there will be a table specifically for EOS students. You may get your food only after all the other students have gotten theirs. Finally, you are no longer permitted to participate in any clubs, organizations or sports related to this school."

Paivi sucked in a hard breath. It's not that she didn't know it was coming; it still pained her to hear it. She snuck a look at Christian. He was sitting straight up in his chair, no expression on his face. She could feel her eyes prickling with tears, but she wouldn't let them come. She wasn't about to give the ATC agents the satisfaction of seeing they had hurt her.

Agent O'Higgins dismissed the students to return to class, following them out into the hallway. Paivi trudged along slowly, wishing a giant hole would appear in the floor, sucking her right in. Or just that she could go home. But that would probably break some rule, causing her to be placed under house arrest. At this rate, maybe that didn't seem like such a bad idea.

Throughout the day, Paivi followed her new rules, sitting at the designated table at the front of the room. Her teachers looked relieved that they didn't need to ask her to move. Sometimes she sat alone, sometimes with one other student. She tried to busy herself by taking notes, or looking at her textbook, if only to avoid the stares. She could feel everyone's eyes on her. None of them appeared to be paying attention to anything but Paivi and her glowing button.

It was with a groan that Paivi entered her sixth hour class. It felt like an eternity since she'd last spoken to Jason. She put her head down and went to her new seat.

Jason reached out and grabbed her wrist as she walked by.

"Hey, Anderson, too good for me now that you're a big star?"

Paivi pulled her hand away and headed to the table she knew had been set up for her. Another boy in the class, Tyler Matthews was already sitting there. She threw herself down into the chair and started to cry. She buried her face in her arms, but didn't much care if people saw her. The tears poured out, hot and angry.

Jason rushed to her, putting his arms around her shoulders.

"I am so sorry, I was just kidding! I swear! I'm sorry! I didn't mean anything by it. I...I don't know what to say. Please!"

Between sobs she attempted to get out a few words.

"I'm...not...allowed...to play...anymore."

She began sobbing harder than ever. The floodgates had opened. All of the tension of the past few days, the shame, the embarrassment, all came rushing out.

"Oh my god! I am so sorry Paivi! I didn't know!" he hugged her in vain, unable to stop the tears.

At that moment, Dr. Hasenpfeffer burst through the door. She dumped her usual pile of books and papers onto the desk and went straight over to Paivi, who was still sobbing uncontrollably.

"Oh you poor thing!" Dr. Hasenpfeffer pushed Jason to the side. She pulled Paivi into a hug, patting her on the back. "There, there sweetie, go ahead and let it all out."

The bell rang. The rest of the class sat awkwardly in their desks, whispering to each other.

"Jason, fill me in," Dr. Hasenpfeffer ordered.

"I, uh, all I did was make a comment about basketball and she started crying. I was able to get only a little of the story out of her. She said something about not playing anymore."

"It's okay Jason, it's not your fault. I'm sure it has to do with this." Still holding Paivi, she grabbed a booklet from the top of her messy pile and handed it to Jason.

He looked at it, slightly bewildered. The title read 'EOS School Policies: How to deal with EOS students.'

"Basically," Dr. Hasenpfeffer continued, "these students, like Paivi and Tyler, are considered Enemies of the State by your future president."

The class sat silently and stared blankly at Dr. Hasenpfeffer.

"Seriously, you guys watch television sometimes, don't you? This past Sunday, December 7th, President-elect Stevens gave a speech. Anybody?" She looked flabbergasted by their silence. "Come on kids, you have to know what's going on around you! Get informed! Okay, Paivi, I'm going to have you sit down, no, in your normal spot please."

She guided Paivi to her desk.

"Tyler, back to your original seat as well. Crystal, close the door. Okay, so no one saw the speech the other night? Well, here's what you missed. This new organization, set up by the government, known as the Anti-Terrorism Coalition, announced that they had knowledge of people suspected in helping the terrorists of the Righteous Front. They released the information in the newspapers yesterday and all of those listed had to show up to a given location to register. They have made these people wear these silver badges to identify them." She gestured to Paivi and Tyler. "They have rules to follow in their daily lives, and according to this booklet, they have even more rules to follow here at school, such as sitting at special tables in their classes and at lunch. They've also been dropped from all activities and sports because of the new, strict curfew laws."

The students remained quiet, taking in the information. A hand went up in the back.

"Dr. Hasenpfeffer," asked James Boggs, a tall, red-haired freshman, "why are they considered 'Enemies of the State?' I mean, what did they do? They must have done something bad."

"That's a fair question, James. That's exactly what they want you to think. Tyler, Paivi, did they tell you what you were charged with?" asked Dr. Hasenpfeffer.

"No," Tyler answered curtly.

Paivi shook her head.

"They said we had to go to some interview, so I guess they will tell us more then. Maybe," said Tyler.

"This, class, goes against these students' constitutional rights. As does being forced to follow these ridiculous school policies," Dr. Hasenpfeffer threw the booklet across the room, banking it off of the wall and into the garbage can. "In this class, I will not make my students subject to rules of these, these…Nazis." She spat out the word. "That is why I have asked them to remain in their usual seats. For your own safety, you may want to keep your little silver buttons on, but I'm not going to turn you in if you don't. We are going to get on with our lesson, but please, more than ever you all need to get informed! This is your life we're talking about here. Wake up people!"

Dr. Hasenpfeffer then turned to the day's lesson, which was something about the Middle East. Paivi was too distracted to pay attention. She could feel the other students' eyes boring into her back the whole period. She could only stare at the clock and will it to move faster.

By the end of the hour, there were doodles in her notebook that she had traced over so many times that she had pressed them into the pages underneath. At long last, the bell rang. Paivi snatched up her things and bolted for the door. Jason was just as quick, catching the back of her backpack.

"Slow down, speedy!" He pulled her backwards as they entered the hallway.

"I wasn't sure you'd want to walk with me," she mumbled.

"Come on, Paivi, I don't really understand what's going on right now with all of this," he gestured to her EOS badge, "but I'm not going to allow some idiot to choose my friends for me."

He grabbed her hand, pulling her closer to his side. Her fingers tingled, making her forget everything for just a moment before she came rushing back to her all too terrible reality.

"I just feel like such a freak," Paivi whispered. She

noticed an ATC agent up ahead that had not been in the group earlier in the morning. She looked at him in disgust.

"It's like they're multiplying," she muttered.

"Who?" Jason asked, and then noticed her staring at the man dressed in black, his badge glowing, silver and bright. "Oh, these guys? I know! It's like they came out of nowhere. Listen, let's just go get some lunch, my treat. I think it's hot cookie day," he tried to make it sound enticing.

Paivi felt like crying for the second time today, remembering the policies. She wanted nothing more than to enjoy a nice lunch with Jason.

"I can't," she sighed. "According to my new rules, I have to sit at a lunch table with the other freaks."

"Stop it, you're not a freak. I guess I'll just have to walk you to your new table and pick you up after lunch is over. In fact," he added, as they entered the crowded lunch room, "why don't I just be your personal security?"

She cracked a smile at the absurdity of it all.

"Aha, there's a smile," he laughed. "No, really, I've always wanted to be a Secret Service agent, well, until Senator Stevens got elected. He's on his own. But in the mean time, I can practice on you!"

"Whatever! You're crazy! I have to find my table."

Maybe it wouldn't be so bad, she thought, if it meant she would get to see him between every class.

Paivi spotted the lone table—it was at the far end of the cafeteria. An ATC guard sat on each end, guarding the four students already sitting there. She could see Christian's blond hair—he was seated in the middle, the furthest he

157

could be from the two guards. At least she wouldn't be alone. As they neared the table, Michaela came running up to meet them.

"Paivi, what are you doing? Are you guys sitting together today?" she smiled.

"No, actually, I have to sit there," Paivi gestured towards the table ahead.

"But why?" Michaela seemed a little annoyed by the information.

"It has to do with this whole thing," Paivi pointed to her badge. "Trust me, I'd much rather sit with you."

She could see one of the agents eyeing her.

"Look, guys, I better go."

Michaela threw her arms around Paivi.

"This sucks! I'll miss you!"

"Don't worry P, we'll come get you at the end of the hour," Jason reminded her.

Michaela unlocked her arms, releasing Paivi from her grip. She gave one last sad look at Paivi and stepped back. Paivi turned without another word and headed to her new table as Jason and Michaela looked on.

Paivi walked by the agent at the end of the table. He looked at her, checking her badge, even though he had already seen it from across the room. He didn't say a word, and didn't offer so much as a smile. She passed by him, her head held high, and chose a seat next to Christian. From there they could see the whole cafeteria. Christian looked up as she sat down. His chemistry homework was spread out in front of him.

"Hi." He didn't sound pleased.

"Hi," she answered. It didn't seem like he was very talkative and she didn't want to push him. She pulled out her paper lunch bag from her backpack. Luckily, she had remembered to bring some food today. Who knows how long it would be until the agents would let them go get lunch.

Paivi opened her bag. Peanut butter and jelly. Bag of chips. Apple. The only thing she hadn't brought was a drink.

"Do you want some of my lunch?" she offered a half of her sandwich to him.

"No thanks," he responded. He shoved his book toward her. "But I could use your help with these chemistry problems."

"But I don't...," she began to protest, preparing to explain that she hadn't had chemistry yet when she saw what was on the notebook paper sitting on top of Christian's open book. In the middle of his homework were the words PAIVI PLEASE JUST READ.

Paivi looked at him.

"Uh, sure I can help you," she glanced back to the page.

"Well, I am mostly having trouble with this number," Christian pointed, touching it with his pencil. The writing jumped to life, like a swarm of ants, rearranging across the page into a new message.

YOU CAN JUST THINK, DON'T SPEAK.

She looked at Christian, and for the first time that day he smiled. She understood. He could read her mind. He touched his pencil to the paper, the words dissolved and reformed.

THEY KNOW ABOUT US.

"These two things go together," she pointed at the paper, trying to keep up the guise that she was helping him with his Chemistry. She glanced at the end of the table, checking out the ATC agents. They were looking around the cafeteria in utter boredom.

What do you mean 'they'?

The message changed again.

ATC.

How do you know that?

She made a face.

I KNOW OTHERS ON LIST.

I don't understand. We're not criminals.

MAYBE.

He smiled again.

"What about this problem? Number three?"

Paivi gave him a dirty look.

Well, we aren't terrorists.

NOT US. MAYBE OTHERS.

By why mess with us. We aren't bothering anyone.

NOT SURE.

"Well, I think you're just kind of dumb. This problem is easy," Paivi tried not to laugh.

MAYBE WE ARE DANGEROUS.

Us? Dangerous? Come on!

Christian shrugged his shoulders.

WE NEED TO STICK TOGETHER.

I suppose. But now you can't blackmail me anymore. It seems that everyone knows my secret thanks to the ATC.

OKAY YOU WIN.

One of the ATC agents suddenly turned around, facing them. Paivi's heart jumped into her throat.

"EOS students," he addressed them. "There will be no lunch for you today."

And with that, he turned back to surveying the lunchroom.

The three students at the other end of the table grumbled to each other. One of them had a lunch that they split. Paivi handed half of her sandwich to Christian.

Here's to sticking together, she thought.

"Thanks," said Christian quietly.

Chapter Fifteen
PA150778

The mood at home was solemn. As bad as her first day back to school had been, she hadn't even thought about what things had been like for Torsten or her parents.

Torsten's day had mirrored her own, with the added bonus that the junior high students were more than prepared to hassle anyone who was slightly different. He had to endure shouts of 'Freak!' as he walked down the hallway, to pennies being thrown at their 'special' table at lunch. The ATC guards at Torsten's school made no effort to stop his harassers.

Mrs. Anderson was informed upon arriving at the St. Andrew Public Library that she was still permitted to work there, but only at the front desk where her supervisors could watch her. Her workday was shortened, as she wasn't allowed to take a lunch break anymore, due to security reasons. Aside from the new policies, Mrs. Anderson found her co-workers to be extremely kind.

Mr. Anderson wasn't so lucky. Upon arriving at the St. Andrew Police Station, he was escorted by a pair of burly ATC agents to the police chief's office. The chief didn't say much, but the ATC agent wasted no time in telling him that he was a security risk and furthermore, a disgrace to his badge. They led him to his locker, forcing him to clean it out, showing them everything as he removed it. Afterwards, they took his badge and gun, and showed him the door, telling him never to return. Aside from a few pitying looks from his former co-workers during the last two hours he spent in the Police Station, no one spoke to him. He was surprised to see, however, that some of his colleagues were wearing ATC badges as well.

"If you can't work, what are we going to do for money?" asked Paivi, looking around at their comfortable kitchen and family room. "Are we going to have to move?"

"No," said Mr. Anderson. "Not right away. We have some savings. I'm going to go to the bank tomorrow. But just be forewarned, no spending money on anything but necessities. Right now that means food and bills. Nothing else."

Paivi and Torsten nodded silently. Mr. Anderson rubbed his face with his hands. Paivi noticed he looked tired and much older than he had just the week before. Their new status as Enemies of the State posed further problems. They needed groceries, but because of the curfew and the shopping restriction, they couldn't go. Mrs. Anderson called the neighbors they had always been friends with, the Cardinellis. Mrs. Cardinelli agreed to run to the grocery store for them after dinner. Paivi was relieved, as was Torsten, as they both had a feeling they wouldn't be getting a chance to buy lunch at school after their experiences the first day back.

The next few days were more challenging at school. The students began to hear more from their parents and from news reports about what the EOS badges meant. The media wasted no time, reporting on what kind of crimes the Enemies of the State might possibly have committed, such as murders of innocent men, women and children and aiding the terrorists by not going to the police. They even speculated as to whether or not they could be responsible for other crimes, from robberies to assassinations. What were curious stares on the first day became worried glances. Most students tried to avoid her, but some felt the need to say things to her, shouting at her in the middle of the hallway.

"Terrorist!"

"Murderer!"

Paivi would generally just put her head down and keep walking. Luckily, she was almost always with Jason, Michaela or Aimee, who seemed to make it their mission to protect her. They would link arms with her and pull her down the hallway, shooting deadly glances at anyone who dared shout at her. On more than one occasion, Paivi had to pull Michaela back as she moved to silence Paivi's harassers. She didn't want anyone to get into trouble because of her and felt lucky enough to have friends that backed her up. Some of the girls, like Jenn Hernandez and Paulina Kaminski, were still nice to Paivi, but didn't seem to want to be seen with her. Crystal Harris, who shared Current Events with Paivi and Jason, explained to Paivi one day after class that her parents had told her under no uncertain terms was she to talk to or hang out with Paivi or any other EOS kids anymore. Not that Paivi was shocked by this news.

"It's okay Crystal, I understand," she said quietly.

Jason arrived at her side, having overheard the exchange.

"Well I don't. Nice friend you are," he snarled at Crystal. "Come on Paivi, you don't need this."

He dragged her off down the hall toward the cafeteria.

"Jason, you don't have to get so mad. It's going to happen," offered Paivi grimly.

"That's the point. It shouldn't happen. Not to you, not to any of these people! I just can't take it! People are so stupid!" He was fuming.

Paivi didn't know what else to say. She had just lost a friend. She didn't feel like losing two. Jason glanced at her and registered the sad look on her face. He put his arm around her.

"Hey, hey, I'm sorry. I know this stuff is hard for you. I'm just so angry that you all have to deal with this garbage. They have no proof that you did anything wrong and yet you're treated like a criminal. And everyone just goes along with all of this blindly, believing whatever their parents say, or whatever they see on T.V.," he paused, "but I have good news for you! Well... maybe."

He turned to her, holding both her hands in his. Her heart fluttered as he looked into her eyes and smiled.

"Paivi, would you go to the Winter Dance with me?"

She looked at him. Her heart was bursting she was so excited. Then realization set in.

"I would love to, but how can I? I can't be involved in any after school activities or anything, plus, there's my curfew."

"See, that's just it, Michaela was able to grab one of those handy little EOS Rulebooks and we noticed that while you can't be involved in clubs or sports, there was no rule about dances. So we went to see Mr. Carson to make sure it was all right, and he said yes. You just have to be home by nine for curfew, but we can still hang out afterwards, if you want. So you can go! Isn't that great?"

Paivi stared at him, stunned.

"You guys did all that and even went to the principal for me? I...uh...I don't know what to say!"

"Saying yes would be a start," he laughed.

"Yes," she sputtered. He squeezed her hands.

"Now, come on, I have to get you to your table before Agent What's-His-Face notices you're missing!" he said as they ran down the hallway, barely clearing the cafeteria doorway as the bell rang. The agent at the table gave them both a dirty look as they walked up. Jason looked at him and smiled. The agent looked disgusted at the sight of them together.

"Have a nice lunch, Paivi," he said, waiting for her to sit down before walking away.

After lunch, Michaela ordered Paivi to go dress shopping with her on Saturday. After all, the dance was only two weeks away, so they had to hurry. Michaela was going with Dan, a guy in her English class, who she described as 'dreamy.' The rest of the week passed quickly, despite the daily torment at school. With Jason and Michaela at her side, she felt relatively comfortable. Her teachers were still nice to her, mostly just giving her pitying looks. Dr. Hasenpfeffer made every effort to treat Paivi normally, continuing to insist that she stay in her old seat.

As they sat in class on Friday, Dr. Hasenpfeffer discussed the European economy. Paivi doodled in her notebook and thought about her lunch.

Ugh, she thought, not turkey again. What I wouldn't do for some chicken nuggets or a slice of pizza.

The door to the classroom was thrown open, startling everyone out of their daydreams. Agent O'Higgins stormed through the doorway followed by two more agents.

"Can I ask why you are disturbing my lesson, sir?" Dr. Hasenpfeffer inquired curtly, unfazed by the intrusion of three burly agents with their glowing badges and guns.

"We've had a report about this class," stated Agent O'Higgins as he strolled through the aisles, looking at all of the students closely.

Dr. Hasenpfeffer remained silent, but looked extremely angry.

"These two students," he pointed at Paivi and Tyler Matthews, "why are they not at the table they are required to sit at?"

"I do not segregate my students, Agent O'Higgins," she answered evenly. "These are their seats and that is where they will sit."

Paivi quickly gathered up her things and started to get up from her seat. Tyler, however, was frozen in his chair.

He looked too scared to move an inch. Dr. Hasenpfeffer was staring at Agent O'Higgins, locked in a defiant gaze.

"Paivi, you sit down in that seat," ordered Dr. Hasenpfeffer, not breaking her lock on Agent O'Higgins. Paivi plopped back down in the chair.

"EOS students are required to sit at these tables and these tables only. Teachers are not allowed to alter those requirements on a whim," he responded coolly. "Now go to the table."

Paivi jumped up and this time so did Tyler. They didn't move more than an inch before Dr. Hasenpfeffer returned fire.

"You will stay in your seats!" she shouted. "That is an order!"

Paivi and Tyler dropped back into their seats, confused and wide-eyed.

"And as for you, Agent O'Higgins, leave my classroom at once."

Agent O'Higgins chuckled. He spoke slowly, but clearly.

"I'm afraid you don't quite have the authority you think you do. One has to appreciate your passion regarding this…trash." He waved his hand in Paivi and Tyler's direction. He gave a nod to the two other agents by the door. They moved swiftly towards Dr. Hasenpfeffer.

"You have broken the law by violating the policies regarding Enemies of the State. The government is forced to believe that you have some reason for protecting EOS students, who are considered criminals. Thus, you must be a criminal as well," he concluded.

He began to read her her rights.

"You have the right to remain silent," he began. The other two agents grabbed Dr. Hasenpfeffer by the arms and forced her to the floor, face down. The class looked on, jaws dropped, frozen in shock and fear.

Paivi jumped up out of her seat, turning to Agent O'Higgins.

"Please let her go! I'll go sit at the table! Please!" she pleaded.

"You and the other one will go sit at the table," he said coldly.

Paivi and Tyler rushed to the front of the room and sat down.

"However, she's still going to jail. She broke the law."

Jason jumped out of seat, getting in front of Agent O'Higgins.

"You can't do this! We have rights! This is illegal!"

"Not any more. Now if you know what's good for you, you'll shut up and mind your own business, or you'll end up like your courageous teacher." He laughed as he pushed past Jason.

Dr. Hasenpfeffer was still struggling between the two agents, who had put her in handcuffs.

Jason turned to face Agent O'Higgins' back.

"She is courageous. And you're nothing but a coward with a badge and a gun."

Agent O'Higgins turned around quickly, his arm

moving in one fluid motion with the rest of his body. His fist landed on Jason's left eye, throwing him sprawling across the desks and students. Dr. Hasenpfeffer flew into a rage.

"You can't do that! You can't assault our students!" she screamed, kicking the larger agent in the shin.

Agent O'Higgins turned towards Dr. Hasenpfeffer. His fist connected with the back of her head, sending her into a crumpled heap on the floor, unconscious. A few of the girls, including Paivi, cried out, but were too terrified to move.

"I think you've all learned a valuable lesson today." He motioned to the other agents. "Let's go."

They picked up Dr. Hasenpfeffer's limp body off of the floor and dragged her out the door, which slammed shut behind them. The students all sat silent for a moment, staring at each other, not quite sure what had just happened. Jason was lying across a desk, holding his face. When he pulled his hands away blood ran from his nose and down his chin, spreading a bright red stain across his shirt. His eye appeared to be swelling fast. Paivi ran over, helping him off the top of the desks. Crystal helped her get Jason into a seat.

"We need to get him to the office. Paivi, he needs the nurse," said Crystal frantically.

Paivi didn't answer. She helped Jason to his feet and pushed him towards the door. She could hear the class muttering, some kids were still crying, but she could hear the others.

"...all their fault."

"...maybe they shouldn't be allowed in school..."

"...I can't believe we have to be in class with them. It's too dangerous."

"Wait until my parents hear about this!"

She stopped at the door and turned back, seeing Tyler still sitting at the table, staring off into space. She couldn't just leave him there. It was too hostile.

"Hey, Tyler, come on, I could use some help."

He jumped up, startled and joined them at the door.

"Let's go."

They walked quickly down the hallway towards the main office. Paivi had her arm around Jason, and Tyler was on the opposite side, not sure what to do.

"Why did you make me come with you?" Tyler asked.

"They were pretty mad and I was worried what they might do to you if you stayed."

They turned into the main hallway.

"They blame us for this, you know," she added.

Through the main entrance they could see black cars parked in the front drive, with numerous ATC agents milling around. She didn't see Dr. Hasenpfeffer anywhere.

At that moment, Principal Carson came storming through the front doors. Ms. Merriweather rushed behind, trying to keep up.

"I will have that man's badge, I tell you! Assaulting and arresting one of our most senior teachers! It's bad enough we have to put up with them milling around and enforcing their 'policies', but they have to behave like tyrants as well?"

He spotted Paivi, Jason and Tyler stumbling down the hallway. Noticing Jason's bloodied face he asked, "And what happened to him?"

"Agent O'Higgins," Paivi answered.

"That's it!" he shouted, causing Ms. Merriweather to jump. "I want that man out of this building! He's a menace! Now he's attacking the students! Get that boy to the nurse's office and when he's taken care of, I'll see you three in my office."

Paivi and Tyler rushed Jason past the startled secretaries and into the nurse's office. The nurse, Mrs. Moeller, jumped up from her desk, dropping her copy of Glitz magazine, and ran over to them.

"Oh my, what happened to him?" she asked, helping him to the nearest chair.

"Agent O'Higgins punched him in the face," offered Tyler.

"My word! All right, let's move your hands out of the way, I need to see what you've got going on here." The nurse lowered his hands. Jason's right eye had swollen completely shut and was a bright purple. At least his nose had ceased gushing blood, leaving a trail of dried blood behind. Paivi gasped and looked away.

"Oh my," Mrs. Moeller clucked. "You're going to need to go to the hospital for an x-ray. I want them to make sure nothing is broken in there."

Jason groaned and looked towards Paivi.

"Am I really that hideous? You'll still go to the dance with me, right?" he attempted to crack a smile.

She almost smiled, but then remembered the events that had put them in the nurse's office.

"Shut up! This is very serious." She sat down next to him. "At least it's temporary ugliness. Maybe it'll look better by the dance."

Tyler joined them, not saying anything. Mrs. Moeller returned with some gauze and antiseptic to clean the blood off of Jason's face, and a bag of ice for his eye.

"Here you are, you poor thing," she fawned over him, wiping his nose and chin. "Now put this ice on your eye, we've go to stop that swelling right away. I called your mother as well. She'll be in to pick you up in a little bit and take you to the hospital."

Jason groaned and Paivi wasn't sure if it was because his mom was coming or from the pain of putting the ice over his eye.

Ms. Merriweather popped in the door, startling them.

"Mr. Carson wants to see you three right away." She looked to Mrs. Moeller for consent. "Is he okay to go?"

"Yes, just keep that ice on your eye!" Mrs. Moeller ordered Jason.

He rolled his one good eye.

They made their way through the main office following Ms. Merriweather to the principal's door. She knocked lightly and heard him answer.

"Come in." Mr. Carson eyed them as they entered.

They took a seat in the chairs in front of his desk. He was no longer as agitated as before. Instead, he slumped in the chair and ran his hands through his thinning blond hair.

"Normally I would have you kids in here, ask what happened, you know, get both sides of the story," he muttered.

"But it doesn't matter this time. No matter what you tell me, we're still wrong. No matter that an agent of a governmental department has been able to segregate my students, physically attack them, and assault and arrest one of my own teachers. Despite all of that, we are the ones who are in the wrong. We could possibly be punished. We are the bad guys!" he shouted, slamming a fist hard on his desktop.

Ms. Merriweather looked a bit shocked, but said nothing. Paivi glanced quickly at Jason and Tyler. They both looked as uncomfortable as she felt, unsure of what to think of Mr. Carson's words.

"Now here's what's going to happen. Because of this incident, the ATC intends to send more agents to our school and allow some of our students to join a group called the YATC. The Youth Anti-Terrorism Coalition. They'll be helping the ATC agents. As if we need more of these goons patrolling our halls. If there is another incident like today, they will kick us both out, Ms. Merriweather, and install Agent O'Higgins as the principal." Mr. Carson leaned back in his chair, gripping the armrests until his knuckles turned white.

Ms. Merriweather eyes welled with tears that threatened to spill down her cheeks.

"I really want to help you and protect my students, but according to the ATC, that's against the law." His voice got quiet again. He looked at them carefully, brimming with desperation. "I can't help you. You kids are on your own against these people. All I can say is do your best to follow the rules and steer clear of those guards. I wish it wasn't this way."

"I'm really sorry," offered Paivi quietly.

"There's nothing to be sorry about, Paivi. I'm proud of you kids for standing up for what you know is right. At the moment, however, right is wrong, and there doesn't seem to be much we can do about it."

He rose from his chair.

"You can go for the day. Pick up passes to leave the building from Mrs. Medina. Just try to stay under the radar here at school for the next couple of days."

As they exited the principal's office, they stopped by the stern looking secretary's desk to receive their passes. Heading towards the front of the main office, Paivi noticed a woman with dark hair sitting nervously on one of the chairs in the waiting area. She jumped from her seat as they approached.

"What on earth did they do to you?" she shouted, rushing over to Jason and pulling the ice pack from his eye.

She gasped.

"Oh, my poor baby!"

She wrapped him in a big hug, which was difficult, because she was so much smaller than Jason. He looked mortified. After disentangling himself from the woman's embrace, Jason turned to Paivi and Tyler.

"Um, this is my mom."

"Hi there, you poor things. The nurse told me what happened. Thank you for helping my son."

"Oh, it's okay, really," said Paivi. She worried Jason's mother might be angry with them, but she did not appear to be in the least.

"We better get you to the hospital, I want them to make sure nothing is broken," said Mrs. Santos.

"Fine," Jason sounded exasperated. "Can Paivi come with us? It's okay, we're allowed to leave, the principal gave us permission."

He held up his yellow pass.

"Yes, of course." Mrs. Santos turned to Tyler. "Would you like a ride home, dear?"

"Um, no, but thank you. I just live down the block," Tyler answered sheepishly.

The ride to St. Andrew Hospital was short and as was the wait in the emergency room. While Jason was taken for x-rays, Mrs. Santos made small talk with Paivi, mostly regarding the latest movies. Finally, they were asked to the small examining room where Jason waited with the doctor.

"According to the X-rays, your son does not have any broken bones in his face," the doctor said, holding up the black and white film. He smiled at Jason's mother, but when he turned to Paivi, he looked straight at her EOS badge and his smile faded. "I am prescribing him medicine for the swelling and the pain, and he should probably stay home from school tomorrow."

He wished them a good day and then left them to collect Jason's belongings. Paivi looked at Jason's swollen and bruised face. She felt so awful. This was all her fault. She couldn't understand why Jason and Mrs. Santos were so nice about it. On the ride home, Paivi was quiet, just listening to Jason and Mrs. Santos talk as they drove across town. She spoke only to give them directions to her house.

It was dusk when they pulled up in front of Paivi's house. She was happy to be home, taking in the wide, welcoming front porch. Her mother had left the lights on, which shone warmly against the red brick exterior. Paivi spotted something bright on the lawn, but it was blocked from her view by a large maple tree. She could see it was glowing, but from the angle, she couldn't tell what it was. When they pulled into the driveway, she could see it clearly. A large sign, containing three glowing letters spelling out 'EOS,' and four sets of numbers, including a number she recognized from her own EOS badge, stood next to the front walk. She could feel her cheeks burning.

"I better go. Sorry about today." Her voice was barely louder than a whisper. She grabbed the door handle to let herself out of the car.

"They really have gone too far," scolded Mrs. Santos. "They should be ashamed of what they're doing to good citizens." She gestured to the sign. "Paivi, you take care of yourself," she added.

"Okay," Paivi's voice squeaked as she jumped out of the car and headed for the front door. She pushed the door open and headed for the kitchen. Mr. Anderson was sitting in front of the television. Paivi added her EOS badge to the charging device on the counter, where three badges already sat, glowing in unison. The device beeped, and a small light next to the badge switched from red to green. Paivi figured Torsten and her mother must be upstairs.

She plopped down on the couch next to Mr. Anderson, hoping he wouldn't ask her how her day was or why she was home so close to curfew.

"So, how was your day?" he asked.

"It was fine."

It was much better to say that than to go through the horrid details.

"I happened to get a phone call from your principal today," Mr. Anderson added nonchalantly, giving her a sideways glance.

Paivi groaned, hiding her face in her hands.

"He told me everything. How's your friends face?" he inquired.

She lifted her head.

"Nothing was broken, at least."

"Well, that's good. What they did today, your friend and your teacher, was very courageous. Some might say stupid, considering the current attitude of the government. Those ATC agents run everything. And they're everywhere—I see them trolling the neighborhoods and your mother said they are on patrol all over town. I hope that they go easy on your teacher. I wish there was something we could do to help her. Someday, when this all passes, I would like to shake her hand. She's a good person, that Dr. Hasenpfeffer. Your friend Jason too."

Paivi shook her head in agreement, not sure what to

say.

"Now, Paivi, I haven't said anything so far, but I just want to remind you to please be on your best behavior at school. Follow every rule in that policy book. I had the same talk with your brother, too. Those ATC agents seem to be looking for any excuse to harass people, and I don't want them to have any reason to hurt you like they did to those nice people today."

"Okay Dad." Paivi was too drained from the day's events to argue that she had done everything possible to avoid trouble.

Mr. Anderson stood up from the couch suddenly.

"Come with me, I want to show you something."

Paivi got up and followed her father upstairs to the loft. The room used to be a playroom for Paivi and Torsten when they were younger and had since been transformed into a den with some overstuffed chairs and a wall of bookcases.

"I already showed your mother and brother," said Mr. Anderson. "You know I've had a little time on my hands, being fired and all," he added bitterly, "and with everything going on, I didn't trust the ATC not to freeze our bank accounts. So I took all of the money out and I hid it here." He gestured toward the wall of bookcases. "I want you to know where it is in case anything happens to us and you need it."

"Oh, Daddy, come on, nothing is going to happen to you." Paivi tried to hide her fears and forced herself to sound reassuring.

"I took a few books from the bookcase and hollowed them out. I hid the money inside."

He pulled four hardcover books from the hundreds of books on the shelves. <u>Heart of Darkness.</u> <u>The Scarlet Letter</u>. <u>Utopia</u>. <u>1984</u>. He opened the covers. Each book had a rectangle carved into the center. In the rectangle was a pouch, which he opened and showed her the bundle of cash it held. "I didn't glue the pages together because I still wanted it to look like a normal book all the way around. Anyways, memorize the titles in case you need them, okay?"

He returned the books to their spots.

Paivi was impressed by her Dad's workmanship but she hoped its purpose would never be necessary.

Chapter Sixteen
Phase Two

Paivi Anderson
Current Events p.6
Mr. Finch

I read an article in the St. Andrew Herald by Mimi Snodgrass titled 'St Andrew Herald reporter Jerome Knowles arrested by ATC.' Mr. Knowles was arrested Saturday for using the newspaper to turn citizens against the ATC. They also found that he commonly associated with people in St. Andrew known to be Enemies of the State and felt that he could be using his access at the newspaper to aid terrorists. Fellow reporters stated that Knowles was known to be a troublemaker and that they were not surprised. I was surprised too, because I always thought he was a good reporter who always stuck to the facts. I guess I didn't really know what he was like at work, but it's really too bad he was arrested.

Ms. Anderson, you should concern yourself with more significant matters, such as how the ATC program has been a success or the drop in terrorist attacks and not

about criminals. Very weak.
D

President-elect Wendell Stevens sat in his sunny breakfast room, a cup of coffee in one hand and the Washington Post in the other. A plate of half-eaten fried eggs and bacon sat in front of him. He set the cup down and placed a forkful of eggs into his mouth.

Nancy, his maid, interrupted his quiet meal.

"Sir," she said quietly, "General Kobayashi is here to see you."

Stevens swallowed his eggs.

"Please show him into the study, Nancy. I will be there shortly."

She nodded and exited the room. Stevens quickly emptied his plate and grabbed his cup of coffee. He adjusted his robe, which he wore over a pair of flannel pajamas, and made his way to the study. He took a seat in a large leather armchair at a mahogany desk across from his visitor.

"Good morning, Michael. Coffee?" he greeted the general, who sat before him in civilian clothing.

"Yes sir. Thank you."

Nancy was hovering in the doorway and scurried to the kitchen, having overheard the request.

"This is an early visit," he commented.

"Yes, sir, well I have some excellent news to share with you and I felt it was best to come right away." The general sounded delighted.

"Fantastic. I can't argue with good news in the

morning. Please, carry on," he encouraged.

Nancy reentered the room and placed a tray with a white coffee mug, sugar dish, and a pitcher of cream onto the desk. She left the room as silently as she came, closing the doors noiselessly behind her. General Kobayashi spooned some sugar into his cup—two spoonfuls—and a dash of cream. He took a sip.

"Perfect. So, I am happy to report, I just flew back form the Phase Two project. Celine showed me around. The facility is complete, a full month ahead of schedule. It can start receiving shipments as soon as Foster and Haley are ready to process them." He took another long sip of coffee.

"Excellent. And the press releases?" he questioned.

"They're set to go out next week. We'll have small blurbs in the national press, mentioning the need to detain Enemies of the State for questioning—for the security of the nation, of course. Locally we'll throw in some extra warnings about extremely dangerous criminals being kept at the Phase Two facility, so the civilians will keep their distance," reported General Kobayashi.

Stevens rose, clapping the general on the back as he walked toward the window.

"Good man. It's a great thing you are doing for your country. Your contributions to this great land will live long after us! Say, it's warm enough out there today, what do you say, why don't we hit the driving range?"

183

Chapter Seventeen
Winter Wonderland

Paivi returned to school the next day after the incident in Dr. Hasenpfeffer's class. She tried her best to do as her father had asked. She flipped through the EOS policy book, making sure she was following all of the rules correctly. She moved quickly and quietly through the halls, dragging Jason or Michaela by the arm. She didn't want to be late for classes, especially not for lunch. She tried to keep to herself in class, and didn't raise her hand or ask any questions. She would respond politely, if ever a teacher asked her a question, which was very seldom. She wished she wasn't there, that no one could see her. Oh, to be invisible!

As for Dr. Hasenpfeffer's class, Paivi dreaded going there the most. Instead of open and friendly, the class had taken on a dreary atmosphere, as if someone had died. They were not told where Dr. Hasenpfeffer was or when she would return. Instead, they had the ultimate pleasure of being taught by Mr. Finch, a squidgy looking substitute teacher in his twenties who bored them to death with his endless lectures. Paivi sat with Tyler at her assigned EOS table and attempted to avoid everyone's eyes for the long fifty minutes of class. She could feel them anyways.

There was a buzz in the hallways as students noticed the signs advertising the Youth Anti-Terrorism Coalition. Paivi heard students talking about the possibility of joining the group and shuddered. Kids with power did not sound like another ingredient she wanted to add to the already bitter soup of her life.

At least she did have the dance to look forward to, although she wasn't quite sure she even wanted to be out in public anymore. It had been nearly impossible to even get the dress.

Paivi had gone with Michaela the previous Sunday to the dress shops in downtown St. Andrew to look for the perfect gown. She had a strict budget from her father, but her mother had slipped her a few extra bills when she hugged Paivi goodbye. They made every effort to avoid the ATC agents that wandered in packs through the streets of downtown St. Andrew.

They first headed to Nora's Boutique. The weather had been cold and snowy all week, making the days a constant shade of gray. The warmth hit their frosty cheeks as they pulled open the door. The rows of colorful dresses brightened the dull day. Before they could get very far, a plump lady with a head of curly, gray hair held back in clips approached them.

"I'm sorry girls," she said quietly, trying not to be overheard by the other customers. "But you'll have to leave."

"Excuse me?" responded Michaela loudly, causing the other patrons to turn and look at them.

Paivi burned with embarrassment, her cheeks turning a deep red.

"Why?" demanded an angry Michaela.

"Well, it's not my rule, but people with those," she pointed at Paivi's glowing EOS badge, "are not allowed in here."

Paivi could feel the customers staring at her. She looked at the floor.

"That's fine. I wouldn't shop in this dump anyways!" shouted Michaela as heads turned towards them. She grabbed Paivi's arm and pulled her out the door, making sure to slam it on the way out.

Despite the streets of downtown St. Andrew being decorated for Christmas, Paivi couldn't quite feel the same holiday cheer as she had in the past. The lampposts were dressed with evergreen garland and bright white twinkle lights. Shop windows sported wreaths and bright red ribbons, along with Santa Claus and his many reindeer. Paivi walked quietly down the street, glancing at the shops as they passed. She failed to notice the elaborate decorations—all she could see were the white signs with red lettering posted in every door and window that carried no holiday goodwill.

NO EOS ALLOWED

"Paivi, don't let it bother you," Michaela pleaded, trying to salvage the fun they were supposed to be having. "Come on, forget this—let's go have a shake at Al's."

"Alright," Paivi brightened slightly.

They turned the corner and walked down to the entrance of Al's Café. Affixed to the door was the same sign posted in all the other shops.

NO EOS ALLOWED

Paivi's face fell. This was insane. All of her favorite places didn't want her there. And for what? She had done nothing to deserve being treated like a second-class citizen. Shame and self-pity was now gone, replaced by anger that she could feel welling up deep inside.

"Let's just go home," Paivi muttered through clenched teeth.

Paivi resigned herself to wear an old dress. What else could she do? On Monday at school she even thought about telling Jason that she wanted to skip the dance, but she didn't want to hurt his and Michaela's feelings after all the effort they made to make sure she could go in the first place.

That night after dinner, Paivi was sitting in the family room with Mr. Anderson and Torsten. The Chicago Bulls were playing Boston. Despite the exciting game, they were all rather subdued. The doorbell rang and Mrs. Anderson called from the living room where she was cleaning.

"I'll get it!"

Paivi could hear a flurry of activity from the front door.

"Hi Mrs. Anderson!" Paivi heard Michaela's loud voice drifting down the hallway. "You remember Jason. He's taking Paivi to the dance, you know!"

What were they doing here on a Monday night? she

wondered to herself.

She decided to see what all the commotion was about. Paivi entered the living room and couldn't believe her eyes. Michaela was laying out ten very different formal dresses that she had pulled out of a large garment bag. Some were long and some short. Some were full of sparkles and some were made of soft velvet. Jason saw Paivi and smiled, and Michaela wheeled around.

"Well, you couldn't go to the dress shop, so we brought the dress shop to you!" Michaela clapped her hands in excitement.

"I can't believe it!" Paivi stammered. "How did you manage this?"

"Jason's sister is friends with the girl whose mom owns Destiny's Bridal. Anyways, she told them what happened on our shopping trip yesterday. They were upset because they have to enforce the same policy and they don't agree with it. So they let us take a bunch of different dresses in your size for you to try. We just have to drop off whatever you don't pick tomorrow."

Paivi ran over to Michaela and threw her arms around her, hugging her tight.

"You are the best!" she said, trying to push down the lump in her throat.

"Oh my god, you're squeezing me to death!" Michaela's voice was muffled by Paivi's shoulder. "It wasn't just me. Jason helped too. We had to pick out some dresses we thought you would like. We made a bet on whose dress you're going to pick!"

"Michaela's choices have no chance," laughed Jason.

Paivi walked over to him, blushing and giving him an awkward hug.

"Thank you so much," she whispered.

"If you are taking Paivi to the dance, you can't see the dresses on her now! I'll take you into the family room, you can watch the game with the boys." Their voices faded as Mrs. Anderson led Jason down the hall to the family room. "Would you like something to drink?"

After two hours of trying every dress on multiple times, they had chosen THE dress. She didn't want to take it off. It was long and light green and accented her eyes. She loved how it sparkled and could picture how it would look in the lights on the dance floor.

Friday was the last day of school before Winter Break and the day before the Winter Wonderland dance. It was quite festive as most of the students were celebrating the holidays. The hallways were full of red and green and brightly wrapped gifts and candy canes were passed around. Paivi, short on cash and barred from all stores but the supermarket, had nothing to give. Not that she had many friends left. Michaela, Jason, Aimee, Christian. A short list. She spent the evening before creating Christmas cards out of paper, ribbons and her very own artwork so she wouldn't be empty-handed. She still felt like it wasn't enough.

Michaela, Jason, and Aimee reacted generously to the cards. Aimee and Michaela gave Paivi small gifts, which she thanked them for. Secretly, she was happier with the fact that she still had a few friends to receive gifts from. To her, their friendship was more important than anything they could give her.

Christian was not as excited about Paivi's card, which she delivered to him at lunch.

"Gee, thanks." His voice was monotone. "Let me give you...oh wait, I can't go buy you anything."

He looked annoyed.

"Ah, don't be such a Grinch," Paivi chuckled.

"You tell me Paivi, just what is there to be excited about? Christmas? Um, no. None of us can go to any stores, so there won't be any presents this year. And as for Winter Break, it's even worse. It's cold and we aren't allowed into...well, anything! No movies, no restaurants, no bowling. So it's going to be like being grounded for two whole weeks. Frankly, I'd rather just be at school, even if it means seeing my favorite ATC agents."

He was out of breath after his tirade.

Paivi sighed, throwing her arm around his shoulder and giving it a squeeze. Boy, how things had changed in the few months since she had met Christian. She used to hate him, and now she just felt sorry for him. He was a sad remnant of the Christian Nelson who had ruled the school. His entourage hadn't stuck around after the list came out, and aside from Paivi, he had no one.

"Don't worry, we'll think of something to do. We can all hang out, watch a movie at my house or something. I'll call you. And at least there's the dance tomorrow. Are you going?"

"No." Christian stood up as the bell rang. "And neither should you."

He stomped angrily out the door.

After school Paivi came home to an empty house. She was confused. Both of her parents' cars were in the driveway, but neither of their badges were on the monitor. She tried not to read too much into it and decided to occupy herself by painting her nails a deep shade of red for the dance.

Torsten arrived home not long after Paivi.

"I don't remember them saying anything about going out," he said as he joined her in the family room, flipping on the television. "God, that stuff stinks. I don't know why you girls have to do paint your fingernails anyways."

They began feeling restless as the clock hands crept closer to five. Paivi repeatedly walked to the foyer and looked out the front window, checking for any sign of her parents. Torsten's eyes flicked back and forth from the clock to the EOS badge monitor as if waiting for it to react to the fact that it was still missing two badges.

The clock struck five. The monitor remained silent.

"Paivi," Torsten whined nervously. "It's after curfew. Where are they? What should we do?"

Paivi wanted to cry; she could feel the lump growing in her throat. She sat down next to Torsten and put her arm around him, hugging him. He was her little brother and she needed to act like the big sister.

"I'm going to give Mrs. Cardinelli a call. Maybe she talked to them."

She picked up after one ring.

"Hi, it's Paivi."

"Oh, hi dear, how are you?"

"I'm okay Mrs. C. Um, I was wondering if you might know where my parents are?"

She bit her lip, hoping for an explanation.

"What?" Mrs. Cardinelli's voice sounded alarmed. "It's after five. You mean they aren't there?"

"No, the cars are here, but the house was empty and there was no note or anything. I thought maybe you had talked to them?" Paivi's knees felt weak.

"Well, I spoke to your Mom earlier, they had sent her home from work. But then I left to run some errands and I just got home. Look, why don't I come over, I don't want you kids sitting there alone."

"Oh, Mrs. C., you don't have to do that." Paivi didn't want to impose, although secretly she hoped Mrs. Cardinelli would come.

"Are you sure, sweetie?" she asked.

"Well, maybe later, if they still aren't here. I just don't want to ruin your night."

"Oh, nonsense! Let's do this, I'll give the kids dinner and then get them off to bed. If they still aren't home by nine, I'll come over and stay with you until they show up. I'm not leaving you poor kids alone overnight. And Mr. C. will hang out here, just in case they call. Be sure to call me if they come home, otherwise, see you at nine."

"Okay, Mrs. C. Thank you so much."

Paivi hung up and went to sit on the couch. She was there only a few minutes before she jumped up and wandered around aimlessly. She couldn't sit still. On she paced, along with a nervous Torsten, watching the crawling hands of the clock.

At last it was nine o'clock. The doorbell rang and Paivi ran to open it, thrilled to see Mrs. Cardinelli, but feeling a bit sicker inside because it wasn't her parents.

Mrs. Cardinelli held out her arms towards Paivi and she gladly accepted the hug. The Andersons had known the Cardinellis for many years; Paivi didn't remember a time when they weren't a part of her life. Mrs. Cardinelli was the next best thing to having her own mother there. She tried for a while to take their minds off their parents, asking them questions about school and friends. The hours continued to tick by and they eventually ran out of conversation. Paivi returned to her aimless pacing, looking out the windows. She walked through rooms turning on just about every light in the house, chasing the shadows out of the corners.

Just before one o'clock in the morning, Paivi finally tired of her routine. She dragged herself down the hall and back into the family room, where Torsten and Mrs. Cardinelli were dozing on the couch. Just as she sank into the chair, she heard the click of the latch on the front door.

"Someone's here!" Paivi shouted to the drowsy pair on the couch as she raced down the hallway.

Mr. and Mrs. Anderson were coming slowly through

the front door. Their faces were ashen, their clothes disheveled, and they had dark circles under their eyes.

"Ohmygodareyouokaywherehaveyoubeen?" The words tumbled out of Paivi's mouth like some kind of verbal waterfall. Paivi threw her arms around them both, tears from all of the stressful waiting poured down her face in relief. Torsten and Mrs. Cardinelli were right behind and joined in the giant hug.

Finally, Mrs. Anderson was able to encourage them all to let go, claiming she couldn't breathe. They moved as a group to the kitchen, where they all sat down at the large table. Mr. and Mrs. Anderson looked exhausted.

"Thank you so much, Vi, for coming to be with the kids." Mrs. Anderson patted her friend's hand across the table.

"Oh, Maria, it's nothing. I should go—I don't want to get in the way." Mrs. Cardinelli rose from the table.

"You can stay, Violette, you know you're family anyways!" Mr. Anderson gestured for her to sit down.

"So, where were you all day?" Torsten was wide-awake now, sitting on the edge of his chair.

"We were with the ATC, at their offices. We were," Mr. Anderson paused, appearing to search for the right word, "questioned. A lot. And for a long time."

Mrs. Anderson began to sob into her hands.

"Did they hurt you, Mom?" Torsten jumped out of his chair, moving to comfort his mother.

Mr. Anderson answered for her.

"Look, we don't need to relive today's events. It's

all over now and we're home safe."

"What are we going to do?" Paivi put her hands on the table. "We should leave. Come on Dad, we have to get out of here."

"No," Mr. Anderson was firm. "If this is what it takes to prove that we are loyal Americans, then that is what we will do. Sometimes, Paivi, you have to take a stand for what you believe is right, even if it is painful. I know we're innocent. We've never hurt anyone. We are good people and I will be damned if I am going to run off like some coward. That just makes them think they were right, that we are some kind of criminals—that we have something to run from. Hopefully things will get better now that they know the truth about us."

Paivi looked down at the table, ashamed. She couldn't understand her father's feelings. Everything in her was telling her to run. But he wouldn't listen. What could she do?

Mr. Anderson stood up, trying to force his voice to sound slightly more cheerful.

"I think it's been a long day for all of us. I could sure use a good night's sleep."

Everyone rose from the table. Torsten helped Mrs. Anderson up; she had finally slowed to sniffles.

"Thank you again, Violette, for looking after the kids. You're a good friend."

"I know you would do the same for me," she replied.

Mr. and Mrs. Anderson hugged Mrs. Cardinelli and walked her to the door. Torsten and Paivi waited for their parents, heading upstairs for a restless night of sleep.

Paivi tossed and turned most of what was left of the night. Towards dawn she drifted into an exhausted sleep.

Suddenly, she was freezing. All around her she could feel an icy wind tearing at her clothes, ripping at her skin. She was barefoot in the snow and was unable to feel her toes. Snowflakes swirled around her head. She wrapped her arms tightly around her body, trying to conserve every bit of warmth.

In front of her lay a dark forest, the trees black in the night. She turned around to find a large body of water, stretching into infinity just behind her. Dark, cold, and silent. The sky was dark—there was no moon, no stars overhead.

She knew she would freeze to death if she stayed there. Her mind was numb, too frozen to think. She placed one foot forward into the snow. Maybe if she could do it again, move faster, she could get warmer. So it began, one foot in front of the other, until she paused to look around. The trees had swallowed her. The forest was so dark she couldn't see her hand in front of her face. She didn't know where she was supposed to be going, she just knew she had to keep moving.

One foot in front of the other. Again. Again. Again. Her whole body felt numb now.

Keep moving, she told herself. It won't be long.

Step, step, step through the deep snow. It was up to her knees now.

And then it was there.

A small clearing appeared in the woods; in the

center was a small log cabin. The windows glowed brightly in the darkness sending streams of light into the dark forest. A chimney lazily trailed smoke into the air above.

Paivi instantly felt warmth flow through her, from her head down to her toes. She was so hot—she couldn't understand why the snow around her wasn't melting. She took a few more steps forward, up the wooden front steps and across a wide porch to the front door. She put her hand out to grab the door handle.

Paivi's eyes flew open. She blinked, confused, not believing she was only in her room. Exhausted, she gave up to her tired body and drifted back to sleep.

Paivi awoke at noon, completely panicked due to the fact that she had only five hours to get ready for the dance. Happy that her parents were safe, she put the events of the previous night behind her. Mrs. Anderson and Mrs. Cardinelli had offered to help her with her hair and make-up. After two hours of blow dryers, curling irons, and roughly one hundred bobby pins, her hair was done. It would probably take four days to get it out.

Paivi ran to her room, slipping into her dress and grabbing her shoes. She stopped to look at herself in the mirror. She felt like a princess. But she still needed jewelry. She sprinted to the dresser, she had to find something quick—Jason would be there any minute to pick her up. Paivi opened her jewelry box and dumped the contents out on her dresser. On top of the pile of necklaces and earrings, gleaming in the light of the lamp, sat the ornate box that contained the gold and silver necklace that she had gotten

197

from her parents for her last birthday and popped it open. She picked up the necklace and hooked the clasp around her neck. The locket felt warm against her skin. She grabbed a pair of earrings that caught her eye and shoved them in her ears as she ran down the stairs.

The doorbell rang as she reached the bottom. Mrs. Anderson let Jason in. He was dressed in a black suit with a red and green Christmas-themed tie that pictured elves dancing in a kick line like the Rockettes. The tie glowed with little lights. He looked up at Paivi as she stood on the bottom step.

"Wow Paivi, you look really pretty." He smiled.

"Thanks," she managed as the heat spread through her cheeks.

Mr. and Mrs. Anderson planted Paivi and Jason in front of the fireplace and wouldn't allow them to leave until the camera was full. Paivi made sure to wait until after the pictures to attach her EOS badge to the shoulder strap of her dress. It glowed garishly but at least the red color complimented the holiday theme.

Paivi and Jason finally made there way out to the car, where Jason's older sister, Jessica, was waiting for them. Her dark hair, though much longer, and dark skin resembled that of her brother.

"I was beginning to think I would need to come rescue you!" she teased as they got in the car.

Jessica quickly drove them back to the Santos' house. Due to Paivi's unwelcome status in all shops and restaurants, Mrs. Santos had invited Paivi, Michaela, and

INTO THE SHADOWS

Michaela's date, Dan McIntosh over for dinner before the dance. After another round of pictures and plates piled with steaming hot homemade lasagna, it was back to the car and off to the dance.

Paivi and Jason followed Michaela and Dan down the hall into the gymnasium upon arriving at school. Paivi could hardly believe her eyes, the view was the same as her vision from so long ago. Glittering snowflakes hung from the ceiling, brightly colored Christmas trees sported bright twinkle lights. Giant, gift-wrapped boxes served as seating around the gymnasium's perimeter. Tables with punch and trays full of brightly decorated Christmas cookies stood at the back of the room. The deejay booth stood at the front of the gym, bass pumping out of the speakers and reverberating off the walls.

They had arrived right at seven o'clock, due to Paivi's curfew. They would have to leave at eight thirty in order to ensure that Jessica could get her home by nine. She hoped Jason wasn't too disappointed about having to leave early, but he never mentioned it. With finely dressed students continuing to arrive and the dance floor still pretty empty, Jason and Dan decided a trip to the sweets table was absolutely necessary.

They were standing over the long table, remarking on tray after tray of brightly frosted sugar cookies, some shaped like stars or Christmas trees, when a voice interrupted their cookie discussion.

"Hi Jason." The voice was light, but phony.

Paivi turned to see who owned it and came face to

face with Melissa, Jason's ex-girlfriend.

Ugh, she thought to herself. This can't be good.

"Hi Melissa," Jason greeted her.

"Can I talk to you for a minute?" she requested, keeping her voice polite.

Jason took a bite of the snowman cookie he had picked up.

"Sure."

"Um, in <u>private</u>?" Melissa emphasized the word.

Jason looked thoughtful. Paivi watched him nervously, hoping he wouldn't leave her.

"Um, no." He bit the head off the snowman. "But you could talk to me right here."

A few of Melissa's friends who had been pretending to look at the cookies turned towards them. Michaela and Dan also fell silent, listening carefully to the exchange.

"Are you sure you don't want to reconsider?" Melissa urged, glancing coldly at Paivi.

"Nope. I'm good." Jason casually popped the remainder of the snowman into his mouth.

"Fine then." Melissa seemed to steady herself. Her two friends stepped up behind her, their arms crossed.

"Well," she began, folding her arms over her chest and cocking her head to the side. "I just wanted to make sure you're okay."

"Huh?" Jason appeared surprised at her concern.

"I don't know if you've noticed or not, but you're kind of hanging out with some questionable people. I thought you were, I don't know," she smirked," having a hard time dealing with our breakup."

Jason snorted.

"Excuse me? I'm doing just fine, thanks. And I have no idea what you're talking about."

He folded his arms over his chest and met Melissa's glare. Dan and Michaela stepped up behind Paivi and Jason.

"I was going to see if you'd like to get together sometime? But you'll have to stop hanging around with people like that." She nodded in Paivi's direction.

Paivi bristled, but held her tongue. She had promised her parents she would stay out of trouble. She could feel the energy welling up—so much so that her necklace felt it was burning into her skin. She sucked in a deep breath. As much as she wanted to respond, she couldn't risk and outburst, verbal or otherwise. Instead she remained silent, clenching her fists.

"Really, Melissa, you must be mistaken. I had no intention of going out with you again," he chuckled.

Melissa's face melted in anger and humiliation, going from cute to ugly in a fraction of a second.

"If you really want to continue to associate with a criminal, it's your funeral. And that may not be far from the truth," Melissa pointed at Paivi, "she very well could be a murderer. Have you asked her?"

Jason's eyes narrowed.

"Don't talk about her like that. Where do you come off? You're just jealous."

"Jealous? Of her? Please! At least I don't have to walk around with a giant glowing reminder that I help terrorists. I heard you got beat up by the ATC agents in class last week because of her. You just better hope she doesn't get you killed."

"I know someone who's gonna get killed!" shouted Michaela as she attempted to lunge at Melissa.

Jason grabbed her around the waist, pulling her back so that her flailing arms fell short of Melissa's face. Dan and Paivi stepped in to pull her arms back.

Melissa jumped back, almost knocking over her shocked friends.

"Come on Michaela, we don't want them to throw us out!" Paivi pleaded. "She's not worth it."

"You're right." Michaela glared at Melissa, her eyes daggers. "You're lucky they were here to hold me back. You may not be so lucky next time."

Melissa shrank into her friends, and they dragged her away to the far side of the gym. Luckily, no teachers or ATC agents had witnessed the exchange—they were all milling around near the entrance. Paivi took a deep breath.

In the dark of the gym Paivi noticed a glow coming from the entrance. She looked over to see who was coming in and saw a large group of agents, maybe a dozen, strolling through the door. She tried to get a look at their faces and realized they weren't regular ATC agents. They were faces of students that she saw in the hallway and in her classes every day. There was Henry Blankenship, star of the basketball team, and Mike Howard, Paivi thought he played football. All of them wore the black ATC uniform, with big, black boots. Their badges glowed with the letters YATC.

Youth Anti-Terrorism Coalition. Their recruitment posters had obviously done the job. She was relieved to see that they carried no weapons—just an air of authority—which she worried could be equally dangerous.

Jason followed Paivi's stare.

"They're not exactly dressed in their Christmas best, are they?" he observed. "It's like a pack of Grinches."

Jason was right—the atmosphere in the gym had become more somber. The students spoke a little quieter and pulled their groups a little closer. The boys in black seemed to puff up at the reaction, standing a bit taller and pushing their chests out. The group casually moved out to the dance floor with the crowd.

"I don't know about you guys, but I need a glass of punch before we go out on the dance floor." Jason steered them down to the last table, where they dipped plastic cups into one of the three punch fountains.

A popular song came through the speakers, causing the students still standing along the walls to run for the dance floor.

Jason grabbed Paivi's hand.

"Come on, let's go have some fun!"

Jason, Paivi, Michaela, and Dan made their way to the dance floor, blending in with the mass of bodies moving in rhythm with the music. Another fast song kept the crowd moving. Paivi's favorite slow song came on next. Jason twirled her around, pulling her closer and placing his hands around her waist. She put her arms around his neck. She looked around the room, taking in his closeness and the ambiance of the glittering snowflakes and soft glow of the thousands of twinkle lights. It was so romantic; it was almost possible to forget the incident with Melissa and the YATC convention that seemed to be going on around them. Paivi closed her eyes, holding Jason close and giving him a squeeze, which he returned. She laid her head on his shoulder, breathing in the fresh scent of his cologne.

Opening her eyes, Paivi noticed that the dance floor was rather empty. She pulled back from Jason to get a better view. Couples were leaving the dance floor, some slowly, some more quickly. Paivi could see the YATC students walking through the remainder of the crowd, tapping people on the shoulder and pausing to say a few words. She looked anxiously at Jason's face. His was an expression between anger and sadness.

"What are they doing?" Paivi whispered, biting back tears.

"They're singling us out." His hands tightened their grip on her.

Paivi saw there were a total of five couples left on the dance floor. Of the couples, at least one member of each pair was wearing a red glowing EOS badge. She could see Elena Pappas, her former teammate, dancing with a boy and looking as horrified as Paivi felt.

Around the perimeter of the dance floor, the YATC had split up. As if someone had flipped a switch, they proceeded to turn on their heels towards the walls, their backs turned to them. The crowds of students standing in front of them followed suit. A faceless wall surrounded the entire dance floor. And there was only one opening in the great wall of people—into the hallway that led to the exit.

They wanted them to leave.

The other couples looked confused, and then humiliated as the realization set in and they understood what was expected of them.

"Jason, maybe we should just go," she whispered, wishing she'd seen this in the dream.

"We aren't going anywhere until we've had our slow dance," he said loudly.

"Jason, I'm so sorry," she stammered, her eyes finally overflowing with hot, angry tears that burned down her cheeks. She noticed that Michaela was not on the dance floor and scanned the crowd in panic. She knew Michaela wouldn't have left her without a fight.

"No Paivi," he pulled her back, looking into her eyes, "I'm so sorry, you don't deserve this."

He glanced around the small group at the others, their EOS badges glowing red.

"None of you deserve this."

Jason pulled her close, kissing her softly on the head. She let the sobs loose then, crying into his shoulder.

The other couples moved closer to Jason and Paivi, not wanting to be the first to leave the dance floor. The song came to an end. The deejay didn't start the next song. The gym was silent.

The couples all turned to look at each other. The boy with Elena, a tall red-head Paivi knew named Devon, grabbed Elena's hand and nodded to the others, walking towards the exit. Each couple followed suit. Jason paused and quickly brushed Paivi's tears away with his hand.

"Come on, you can't let them get to you. If you do, then they win."

He grabbed her hand, his chin high, eyes defiant. Paivi attempted to mimic his look, trying to feel defiant or proud, but not feeling like she was succeeding at either.

They exited the gym and could hear the music begin. Jason led her over to the group, trying to figure out how to get home. Jessica wasn't due to pick them up for another forty-five minutes and they didn't feel comfortable waiting until then. Devon and another girl, Sophie, had a car, and the groups agreed to go with whoever lived closest to the driver. Paivi and Jason were to ride home with Devon, Elena, and a girl named Stephanie, while Stephanie's date and the others would go with Sophie.

Paivi felt a strong tap on her shoulder.

She turned to find herself face to face with Michaela, whose face ran with dark streaks of mascara. Her fists were clenched, her body tense.

"Oh my god, Michaela! Are you okay?" Paivi stepped forward, her arms out to embrace her.

"Don't touch me." Michaela's voice was as sharp as a knife. Paivi noticed three YATC boys standing behind her.

"I have to ask you something Paivi."

"Uh, okay," Paivi tried to keep eye contact with her, but Michaela's gaze was piercing.

"Teddy told me something and I want to know if it's true."

A boy in black, Teddy she presumed, smiled smugly and nodded.

"He said his Dad had to interview your parents yesterday."

Michaela took a deep breath, closing her eyes tight and then opening them again. They appeared a little softer and sad.

"He said your parents knew my Mom was going to die; that she was going to have an accident. Is that true, Paivi? Did your parents know?"

Paivi was horrified and speechless. Her brain was so foggy after the events of the evening that she couldn't think of a defense fast enough.

Michaela gasped—taking her silence as an admittance of guilt—and stepped back towards the YATC boys.

"Murderers! Your parents are murderers!" she screamed, her voice cracking.

"Michaela, please, I...," Paivi trailed off, not knowing what to say.

Michaela lunged at her with her whole body, like a cougar pouncing on its prey. Jason was quicker, having anticipated Michaela's attack, and caught her around the waist. She struck him a few times with her fists, only hitting his chest. Devon stepped forward and helped Jason carry her to the three boys in black and set her down on the floor.

She immediately collapsed into a heap screeching like a wounded animal. The sound was piercing, causing everyone around them to cringe. Tears streamed freshly down her face, spreading the mascara like war paint.

Paivi felt sick, she wanted to throw up. This was her fault, completely her fault. She had destroyed her own best friend, who had been so fiercely loyal through this horrible, horrible year.

Michaela was on her knees, tearing at her hair. Her eyes bored into Paivi and she shivered. If looks could kill, she surely would have been dead twice over.

Michaela screamed out again.

"I hate you Paivi Anderson. I HATE you! You're dead to me, DEAD!"

A few teachers came rushing through the door from the gymnasium, headed towards the commotion.

Paivi stumbled backwards, only to find Jason right behind her. He grabbed her arm and dragged her toward the door where the rest of the group was waiting.

Michaela's screams continued to echo through the building and followed them out into the cold, starry night.

Chapter Eighteen

Black

Paivi didn't remember much about the ride home. She spent the entire time sobbing into Jason's shoulder. He walked her up the steps to her front door. On the porch, they stopped for a moment. Both of them were at a loss for words.

"I'll call you tomorrow," Jason whispered into Paivi's ear as he pulled her into his arms. She nodded. He kissed her on the cheek and gave her a squeeze, then walked down the steps back to Devon's waiting car.

Paivi didn't want to remain on the porch, alone in the cold, but she also didn't want to go in. How could she even begin to explain the events of the night? She still felt nauseous and her head hurt from crying so much. She knew she must look a hot mess. She decided it would be best to edit her story. She would have to tell them about Michaela, so they would understand why they weren't friends anymore. And at least that would explain the tears and being home early. But maybe she would leave out the YATC and the incident on the dance floor.

She took a deep breath and opened the front door. At

least she was home. And for the first time, she thought about having to go back to school after two weeks off. Maybe if she told her parents more of the story, maybe she could just be home schooled. She didn't think she could ever face Michaela again.

She walked slowly down the hall into the family room, where Mr. and Mrs. Anderson and Torsten were watching the news on television. She didn't really know how to start. She hoped they would notice her and say something.

Her mother's head popped up fro the couch first, glancing at the clock above the fireplace. She jumped from the couch, trying to take in everything in the dim light of the family room.

"Oh Paivi, you're home early." Mrs. Anderson gasped as she caught sight of Paivi's face. "Oh no sweetie, what happened? You're a mess!"

Mr. Anderson and Torsten opened their mouths, ready to make a joke, but chose otherwise after seeing Paivi's red, puffy eyes. Mrs. Anderson unhooked Paivi's badge and returned it to the monitoring device. She then led Paivi to the couch.

"Here, let's sit down honey, that's it." Mrs. Anderson fluffed the pillow behind her. "Now, please tell us what happened?"

She glared at Mr. Anderson and Torsten.

"I promise they won't say a word."

The boys sat back sheepishly.

Paivi took a deep breath.

"Okay, but don't say anything until I'm done."

They nodded in agreement.

"Here goes…" Paivi leaned back into the couch and looked down at the corsage on the wrist that Jason had given her. She fiddled with the deep crimson ribbon that held the white and red roses together.

Paivi began relaying the events of the evening. She decided to tell it all—she just couldn't hold it all in. After fifteen minutes it was over. She had finished the story, but she didn't feel any better. She looked up, taking in the horrified looks of her family and felt worse.

"Paivi, I am so sorry honey!" Fat little tears rolled down her mother's cheeks. She threw her arms around her daughter.

Mr. Anderson's face went from horrified to livid.

"That's it," he grumbled, "you two are not returning to school after break."

"What!" Torsten squawked.

Paivi felt relieved. The only people she would miss were Jason, and maybe Christian. There was nothing there for her anymore.

"It's not safe for you kids. Those YATC kids are all over the place now. And we already know the school can't protect you, as we saw after what happened to that nice Dr. Hasenpfeffer." Mr. Anderson leaned back into the couch. "You'll be home schooled for now. But I will go to the ATC office and inquire if we can move you out of St. Andrew."

Mr. and Mrs. Anderson appeared to shudder at the mere mention of the ATC office.

"What?!"

Now it was Paivi's turn. She didn't want to go back to school, but leave St. Andrew? She'd lived here her whole life.

"Maria," Mr. Anderson turned to his wife, grasping her small hands in his large ones. "St. Andrew isn't safe for them anymore. It's too close to Chicago, look how strong the ATC has gotten in this area in little more than a month."

Mrs. Anderson continued to cry, but nodded.

"We can see if they can go to Tim and Alissa's. Duluth might be safer because it's much less populated. I'll call them tomorrow."

Duluth! Paivi thought. It was so far from here, and so cold.

"Can't we just stay here, Dad?" Torsten pleaded. "You don't want to go to Minnesota, it's freezing there! It's like the middle of nowhere."

Mr. Anderson thought for a moment.

"As much as we would love to join you in Duluth, the ATC won't let us leave St. Andrew. Their rules appear to be a little more lenient in regards to children. You two would have to go without us."

"But it will only be temporary. It's for your safety," Mrs. Anderson added, trying to sound convincing, but unable to mask her misery. "We'll talk everyday."

"Mom, we don't want to go without you, we don't want to leave our house!" Paivi cried.

"This is the only option right now Paivi, I'm sorry," Mr. Anderson said firmly.

"Paivi, would you please lock the front door for

me?" Mrs. Anderson cleared two cups and a dish from the coffee table. "I'm beat—I think we should all get some rest. We can discuss this further in the morning."

Torsten got up from the couch and straightened out the pillows as Paivi walked slowly down the dark hallway to the front door. As she reached out to turn the deadbolt she heard a loud crunch as the wooden frame shattered and the door flew open. The force of the door hitting her in the face and shoulder knocked her to the ground. She could hear the sound of glass breaking in the family room. Her mother and brother screamed at the same time.

"Mom!" Paivi could barely get the word out.

Within seconds, men in black surrounded her. In the dim light she could see one thing she recognized immediately—the silver glow of their ATC badges. Two of them grabbed her arms, hoisting her off the floor and dragging her down the hallway to the family room.

She struggled to free herself from their grip.

"Let me go!" she screamed at them.

The agent in front of her spun around and slapped her across the face.

"Shut up!" he screamed.

Paivi's eyes welled up with tears and her face stung. She could still feel his hand on her cheek, even though it was no longer there. She could taste blood in her mouth. She squeezed her eyes shut, willing the tears away. She didn't want to give the beast the satisfaction of seeing her cry.

In the family room, Mr. and Mrs. Anderson were on their knees, their faces pushed into the ground by the ATC agents who were putting them in handcuffs. Two more agents had the muzzles of very large guns pointed and the backs of their heads. It appeared there were about ten agents in all—two were holding Torsten in a corner, his face twisted in rage. Two other agents walked around the room, one smashed a crystal vase, throwing it into the fireplace, while his partner chuckled.

"Must be nice to have so many fancy things. I am sure they were all illegally obtained, however, so they'll all have to be confiscated," he ran his fingers across the top of the television, "ATC orders."

Paivi wasn't even listening. She could have cared less about anything in that house. The only thing that mattered was her parents, and making it out of there in one piece.

"Check the badges, make sure we've got the right ones," one of the ATC agents ordered. The men were all quite large—they could have been the defensive line on a pro-football team.

Paivi was shaking, too scared to move.

"The badge numbers are correct."

The ringleader pulled a small black notebook from his breast pocket and flipped it open.

"John Anderson?"

Mr. Anderson didn't answer.

The man with the notebook kicked Mr. Anderson in the ribs. He cried out in pain but didn't move.

"Please, stop!" Mrs. Anderson cried hysterically, trying to rise from the floor.

The agent backhanded Mrs. Anderson across the face. She lost her balance and tipped over.

Paivi seethed with anger. She could feel it coursing through her veins and bit her tongue to try and take her mind off it. But she knew if she said or did anything it would only get worse. "Are you John Anderson?"

Mr. Anderson nodded and whispered, "Yes."

"And you are Maria Anderson?"

Mrs. Anderson was back on her knees.

"Yes."

"I am here to notify you that Mr. John Anderson, EOS number 110838 and Mrs. Maria Anderson, EOS number 110837 are under arrest for the death of Mrs. Luisa Brown, of 469 Oak Street, St. Andrew, Illinois. As an Enemy of the State, you have no right to a lawyer." He nodded to the men standing behind Mr. and Mrs. Anderson. "Take them away."

"Wait!" Paivi cried out, still struggling against the iron grip of her captors. "Please, listen! It was me! It's my fault Mrs. Brown died! Take me instead!"

"No Paivi," Mrs. Anderson cried in horror.

The agent with the notebook laughed.

"Nice try, little girl. You aren't gonna save your parents," he snorted. "No one can."

He waved his hand.

"Let's go."

The two agents behind Mr. and Mrs. Anderson grabbed them by their arms, pulling them to their feet. Mr. and Mrs. Anderson's eyes were glazed with defeat. With the muzzle of their captors' machine guns in their faces, they accepted the fight was over. They were marched through the shattered front door and down the front steps.

Paivi and Torsten were dropped on the floor as the agents followed the group out into the night. They jumped to their feet and followed them outside. In front of the house were five black vans with the white letters 'ATC' painted on the side.

Mrs. Anderson collapsed in the yard, sobbing, unable to move further. The agent that had been holding her arm gave her a kick in the head. She screamed, and giving way to emotion, she jumped up and tried to run towards Paivi and Torsten, who were standing frozen in place on the front steps.

Paivi suddenly sprang to life, leaping off the front steps and running towards her mother. She reached her just as the two agents did, grabbing her mother by the arms. Paivi lunged, grabbing onto her mother, holding on as if her life depended on it. Rather, her life did depend on it. She couldn't see life without her parents.

Torsten reached the group in the middle of the yard, pounding on the arm of one of the agents. The agent flung his arm back, striking Torsten in the face and throwing him to the ground.

"Let go or I'll shoot!" shouted a gruff voice.

Paivi looked up to see the gun pointed at her own head.

"Paivi, I love you. Please do what the man says!" Mrs. Anderson whispered into her ear. She released her grip on Paivi.

"Take care of your brother."

Paivi let go, her knees gave out and she collapsed into the snow. The agents hurried Mrs. Anderson to join her husband at the back of the van, waiting with its black doors open, ready to swallow them. Her parents stepped in gingerly, unbalanced by their handcuffed hands. Paivi looked up and down the street, wishing someone, anyone, would magically appear and come to save them. She was sobbing uncontrollably. The Cardinellis house next door was dark. All of the other homes were brightly lit, and she could see people standing in their windows, watching and doing nothing. Slowly the people in each house, not wanting to be seen eavesdropping, moved away from the windows and turned out their lights. One by one they went dark, leaving Torsten and Paivi alone in their pain on the front lawn.

The instant the van door slammed shut Paivi reacted to the horrible pain burning through her, touching every inch of her. It felt so much more powerful than the anger. She wailed so loud it reverberated off of every house on the street. It came from the deepest part of her soul, now damaged and torn. The vans pulled away, disappearing in a glow of red taillights at the end of the block. She took a deep breath and screamed, this time louder and more tormented. She felt like she was going to explode, every inch of her feeling so hot that her blood was boiling. She was sure she would die. She heard the sounds of glass breaking and the rumbling of an explosion. She opened her eyes, watching as the windows in all of the houses on the street, save the

217

Cardinellis and her own, shattered, blowing out over the lawn as if each house had a bomb in it, set for the same time.

Torsten was at her side.

"Did you do that?" Torsten was in awe.

She managed to find her feet with Torsten's help. Her green dress was torn, face bloodied and her beautifully coiffed hair lie ragged around her face. Paivi's corsage lay in the white snow, crushed by the struggle. All that could be seen was a few of the red petals and what remained of the crimson ribbon.

A light snow had begun to fall, brushing lightly on Paivi's bare shoulders.

"Paivi," Torsten sniffed. "We should go inside. We can't stay out here."

Paivi nodded and he guided her back to the front steps and into the house as she numbly followed. She sat down on the stairs, unable to go any further. Torsten left her there and attempted to secure the damaged doors. He returned to find her sitting, silently staring off into the distance. He wedged himself in next to her on the steps.

"Paivi, what are we gonna do?"

She didn't answer.

There was the sound of sirens in the distance.

"Paivi, please, I need you right now! You've got to figure something out."

"I don't know what to do, Tor." Paivi's voice was barely audible.

Torsten looked at her in anger.

"Mom and Dad are gone, Paivi. We're all alone. We

have to do something. We can't just sit here. And we can't stay here. This isn't home anymore."

She hid her face in her hands. It felt like someone had put her head on upside down and backwards. She couldn't, she didn't want to, wrap her head around the facts. Her parents were gone. How was she supposed to know what to do next?

"Paivi!" Torsten pleaded.

"Torsten!" she screamed back. "I don't know what to do! How am I supposed to decide?"

Her voice echoed through the living room. Torsten shrank back.

"Ahhhh!" she cried out in pain as her neck burned. She grabbed at the necklace, which seemed to be the culprit. It felt like scalding hot water was being poured on her neck and chest. Paivi jumped up from the steps, dancing around, holding the necklace away from her chest. It immediately began to cool.

Paivi noticed, while holding it in front of her that the words on the back of the locket she had gotten from her parents were moving. She looked at it again, unsure if her brain was playing tricks on her after so much stress. It was no mistake—the letters appeared to be floating, like fish in a fish bowl. Some letters were right up against the surface, and some appeared to be floating somewhere deeper in the locket.

"What are you doing?" Torsten jumped up, alarmed. "What are you looking at?"

He stepped next to her, looking at the necklace.

"Whoa! Are those letters moving?"

"I think so."

"What does it mean?"

"I don't know. It's never done this before."

Some of the letters floated closer to each other and raced to the surface.

"YOU," Paivi read the first word aloud.

"MUST," Torsten read, still amazed.

"RUN."

Paivi waited. The letters returned to floating around aimlessly. Paivi shook the locket. They continued to float, some of them bumped into each other.

"Well, where are we supposed to go?" shouted Paivi in frustration.

The next two words popped up quickly.

DON'T SHOUT

"That necklace just told you off!" Torsten laughed.

"Oh, shut up."

The next words came more slowly.

YOU MUST GO TO FRIENDS

"But where please?" Paivi tried to control her voice and be polite to the locket.

NORTH

"North?" Torsten started, confused.

"Oh, north, to Minnesota. That's where Mom and Dad talked about sending us, to Tim and Alissa's in Duluth."

"Paivi, how are we going to get to Duluth? Are we really going to listen to a necklace?"

"Oh, I'm sorry! Do you happen to have any other

ideas? Besides, this appears to be more than just a necklace," she said, shaking the locket at him.

The words swirled around and returned to their original position around the edge of the circle, displaying the Gaelic saying once again.

Paivi's mind was spinning. They had a plan. They had to get to Duluth.

But how?

She started to pace back and froth across the living room.

She topped and looked at Torsten.

"I don't want to stay here tonight."

"Me neither," he agreed. "But where are we going to go?"

"I know, I'm thinking. It said we have to go to friends. Well, the only way we are going to get to Duluth is with help from friends. But which friends?" She rubbed her temples with her fingers. It did nothing to remove the dull ache.

"The Cardinellis aren't home tonight. What other friends are there?" Torsten asked, running his hands through is hair.

Paivi thought for a moment. She didn't have many friends left. In fact, she could only think of two. There was Christian, whom she only recently saw as a friend, because he understood what she was going through. It wasn't safe to go there, though. What if he'd had a similar night? She now had her answer.

"We can't go to Christian's, it wouldn't be safe. But

we could go to Jason's. I trust him. And his mom seemed like she was on our side."

"How far?"

"Three miles or so," she estimated.

"And how are we going to get there?"

"We walk."

Torsten made a face. "Walk three miles in the cold? But it's snowing!"

"Yeah, I got it, but neither of us can drive and our bikes are somewhere in the shed. By the time we get them ready, we could be at Jason's."

"I guess," he conceded.

Paivi began pacing again, thinking aloud.

"We also have to try to get across town without getting stopped. We'll have to stick to the backyards."

She stopped.

"Alright. Go fill up a backpack with what you need. Take warm clothes, but only one backpack. We don't want any ATC agents we come across to think we look suspicious."

They both ran up the stairs. Paivi darted into her room. She grabbed her backpack off the floor, dumping its contents out. She wouldn't be needing her school books anymore. She changed into warmer clothes, leaving the remnants of the once beautiful dress in a heap on the floor.

If I ever come back, she thought, I'll burn it. I never want to remember this night.

Into the backpack went as many pants, sweaters, t-shirts, underwear and socks she could stuff in. In the bathroom she grabbed her toothbrush and a hairbrush. She ran back into her room, remembering one last thing she wanted. From the pile of jewelry that she had dumped out earlier on her dresser, she grabbed the ornate box that had held the locket she still wore. For some reason, she felt she couldn't leave it.

Paivi met Torsten in the loft. They walked over to the bookcase in silence. <u>1984</u>. <u>The Scarlet Letter</u>. <u>Utopia</u>. <u>Heart of Darkness</u>. One by one they pulled the books from their spots on the shelf, opening them to reveal small bundles of money. They each put some in their pockets and in their backpacks. They placed each book gently back in its place.

They stopped in the family room one last time. Paivi took a deep breath and looked around. Torsten was right. It didn't feel like home anymore. She picked up a picture frame that had been knocked to the floor earlier. It was a photo of the family on their last vacation. Those were better days, a beautiful, sunny day on the beach. It seemed like a lifetime ago now. She shoved the frame into her over-stuffed backpack.

"I think we're ready," Paivi put on her winter coat, pulling up the hood. She wound a scarf around her head, covering her nose and mouth.

"Aren't we taking our EOS badges?" Torsten gestured to the device on the kitchen counter where the badges were glowing brightly in the dim light.

"If we can help it, we'll never wear them again. Let's go." Paivi opened the broken back door. "I don't want anyone to see us leave."

Torsten shut the door as best he could and pulled up his hood, tying it tight to keep the wind out. It was snowing lightly—giant, fluffy flakes that floated through the air.

They set off through the backyards, disappearing into the shadows.

Chapter Nineteen
Escape Plan

Paivi wove Torsten through the maze of backyards and alleys, avoiding the main streets until they reached downtown St. Andrew. They needed to cross the river, unfortunately there were only three bridges across and each of them was extremely busy, being the only way over the Fox River for miles around. There was also no chance of hiding in much of the downtown area. They would be completely exposed. Paivi decided they should just act natural, like they had full rights to be out walking around. This wouldn't have been true even if they weren't subject to EOS rules, they were still out past the city curfew.

They had some advantages, however. Paivi and Torsten were both tall for their ages, and what with being bundled up, their young faces were hidden. Also, downtown was also home to the train station and the bus depot, and it wasn't unusual for people to be walking around that area so late at night.

Paivi took a deep breath as they began to cross the bridge. Fat flakes landed on the cement in front of her, adding a clean layer to the pavement. She glanced over the side of the bridge, watching as the snow landed on the swirling water and disappeared as it hit the surface.

Paivi jumped slightly as Torsten whispered her name. She turned to the street and felt her heart drop into the pit of her stomach. Through the snowflakes she could make out the front end of a black car that was driving quite slow as it approached them.

"Keep going," Paivi hissed back at Torsten.

As the car pulled slowly towards them, she was slightly relieved to see the car also had a white stripe and the St. Andrew Police logo on the door, marking it as a police cruiser instead of an ATC vehicle. The car reminded her of her father. She thought back to how he used to give her rides in the police cruiser when she was younger. She thought it was cool to sit behind the bars back then. She pulled herself away from those thoughts—she had to stay focused. The police were far from friends. They could still ask to see identification, which neither of them had.

The police cruiser paused next to them, and the young officer in the passenger seat caught Paivi's eye. Not sure what else to do, she nodded in a polite greeting. Behind the glass, the officer did the same, and they picked up speed, driving up the hill on the other side of the river and out of sight in the now heavy snow.

Paivi sucked in the cold air, realizing she had been holding her breath.

"That was close, Paivi," Torsten whispered.

"It's okay, we'll be there soon."

Paivi and Torsten trudged up the street, the bridge

behind them. They passed Al's Café, Armand's and Nora's Dress Shop. The holiday decorations glittered in the snow. Paivi shivered as she surveyed the scene. She had loved this town. And this would be the last time she would see it for a while. Maybe forever. Torsten was right—St. Andrew wasn't home any more. That had been made that quite clear.

They had reached Jason's neighborhood, however Paivi wasn't as familiar with the backyards and alleys, so they had to go much slower. She wanted to avoid being seen by any of the neighbors. Their efforts were hampered by the thick snow building at their feet.

They finally made their way to Jason's backyard, parking themselves behind the shed. Paivi gave a great sigh of relief and leaned up against the metal wall. They made it.

"Now what, Paivi?" Torsten plopped down in the snow, sitting on his backpack. "How are you going to get lover-boy's attention?"

"Funny. And anyways, there are still plenty of lights on in the house. His room is that one, there, at the back. We can always throw snowballs at the window."

"Wait, look!" Torsten pointed to the back door. "Someone's coming!"

They pressed up against the shed, trying to hide themselves while still attempting to catch a glimpse.

Paivi was immediately relieved to see it was Jason. He had a shovel in hand and was clearing the patio, and oddly enough, some of the grass, of snow. She threw a few snowballs in his direction, all of them falling far short of where he was standing. Before she could get his attention, he disappeared back into the house.

"You missed him, come on!" Torsten whispered angrily. "Just say something!"

Jason returned a minute later, with two dogs on leashes that Paivi had met earlier that night at dinner. A large brown bulldog named Peanut wore a fuzzy pink sweater. The other dog looked like a hamster next to Peanut. It was a tiny Chihuahua named Beast. He wore a black sweater with a skull and crossbones printed on it. Jason walked both dogs to the yard, not fifteen feet from where Paivi and Torsten stood.

Paivi took a deep breath and stepped out from the shadows that hid her.

"Whoa!" Jason jumped back a step. Beast started growling and barking while Peanut tried to drag Jason back to the house, whimpering.

Paivi took another step forward.

Jason squinted, trying to see her clearly in the thick snow.

"It's okay Jason, it's just me, Paivi. Oh, and my brother."

Torsten stepped out from behind Paivi.

"Hi," Torsten offered.

"Oh my god, Paivi! You scared the crap out of me! I thought I might have to tussle with someone!" He took a few jabs at the air with his fists.

Paivi and Torsten moved closer to Jason and the dogs, who had relaxed and ran forward to greet them, jumping on their legs. The light from the porch brightened everything around them.

"Paivi, what happened?" Jason looked closely at her face as they moved into the light. She had tried to clean the blood and makeup off the best she could with a few swipes of a towel before they left the house earlier, but clearly it hadn't done the trick. "Were you in a fight? Are you okay?"

She dropped her eyes, trying to fight the emotions that were welling up inside. Anger, rage, horror, sadness. She pushed them all to the back of her mind.

"They took our parents. We had to leave, and we had nowhere else to go."

"They took your Mom and Dad? Those bastards." Jason's eyes narrowed in anger.

"Look, we don't want to get you or your family in any trouble, we can go. We could just wait out in the shed until morning, if that's all right."

Jason stepped forward and wrapped Paivi in a hug. "You're not going to stay in the shed!" He put his arm around Paivi and patted Torsten's back while still trying to control the dogs as they danced around his feet. "Let's get inside."

Paivi could feel the warmth as they entered the kitchen and due to the layers of clothes, she felt like she was going to suffocate. She slipped her feet out of her wet boots, unwrapped her scarf and took off her hood. She was suddenly embarrassed that she looked such a frightful mess. Paivi and Torsten sat down at the kitchen table after removing their heavy winter coats.

"Do you guys want something warm? I could make

some tea or coffee?" Jason offered.

"Maybe just some water please?" Paivi noticed that her throat ached.

"Ma," Jason called down the hallway, "could you come here please?"

He filled two glasses with water from the faucet and set them down in front of Paivi and Torsten. Paivi took a look at her brother as he eagerly downed his glass of water. She hadn't realized how bruised his face was. He looked terrible.

Mrs. Santos entered the kitchen and noticed Paivi and Torsten right away. She looked slightly embarrassed, as she was already sporting a pair of red flannel pajamas and a pink robe. She looked up again and noticed their faces, and appeared to forget all about her mismatched wardrobe. She crossed the room in one long stride and took Paivi's bruised face in her hands.

"Oh! Honey, what happened?"

Paivi could feel a lump forming in her throat. Her own mother would have reacted in the same way.

"They took our parents," Paivi whispered, fighting back the tears that began to well up. "We didn't have anywhere else to go."

"Well, I am not surprised. Look what's on the news." Mrs. Santos grabbed a remote and turned on the television set that sat on the kitchen counter.

A news anchor sat behind a desk, a picture of a man over her shoulder.

"In addition to the mass round-ups of EOS criminals

that have been in progress nation-wide, there has been a shocking development. Peter Farmington, head of Vantage Tech was arrested earlier this evening at his home in Seattle, Washington on charges of murder and fraud. Let's go to Olivia Krakov for more on this story..."

Mrs. Santos turned the television off. "Even the richest man in the world couldn't save himself. And by the way, you are welcome to stay here as long as you like." Mrs. Santos threw her arms around Paivi.

Paivi took a deep breath.

Mrs. Santos released Paivi and sat down next to her at the kitchen table. Jason took the chair opposite, next to Torsten.

"Thank you for your offer, but we can only stay until tomorrow." Paivi played with her glass of water. "We have to get to Duluth—as soon as possible."

"Duluth Minnesota?" Jason looked surprised. "Why would you want to go there? It's freezing!"

"I know. My parents were talking about sending us there right before they, uh, left." She hesitated. "Torsten and I decided it's where we should go."

"How will you get there?" Mrs. Santos looked concerned. "If you need us too, we could drive you."

"I don't know, but it's too dangerous for you to take us. We're sort of illegal now. We left our EOS badges behind."

Mrs. Santos and Jason looked at them for a moment and then at each other.

"Well, if they're illegal Mom, couldn't we just hide

them here?" He looked at them encouragingly. "Come on, what do you say? We have a really nice basement! You could stay down there."

Mrs. Santos nodded her head in agreement.

Paivi thought about it for a moment, her mind drifting to scenes of her and Jason talking late into the night, watching movies and eating popcorn. It would be like an endless slumber party.

But she had seen the ATC, seen what they could do to a family. The scene in her head changed, to one of Jason's mother being beaten by an ATC guard while Jason looked on, unable to help. She didn't want that for them, however small the possibility. She had not been able to save Mrs. Brown, or her own parents. She would do whatever she could to protect Jason's family.

"No." Paivi was firm. "We appreciate the offer so much, but if they found us here, I know what they would do."

She shivered.

"Well, that still doesn't solve the problem of how you will get to Duluth." Mrs. Santos looked perplexed.

At that moment, Paivi's necklace heated up, burning her neck and chest. She wanted to grab the locket, but she hesitated, unsure what to do. She didn't know if they would understand. But it burned so badly.

Torsten could see her gritting her teeth across the table and grabbing at the chain.

"Just look at it Paivi," he encouraged.

Jason and Mrs. Santos looked at Paivi curiously as

she pulled the locket from under her layers of clothing and flipped it over. The words began breaking apart into the strange alphabet soup. The letters pressed themselves slowly against the lockets surface.

CHRISTIAN

"It says 'Christian.' I don't think it's safe to call him though. Does it mean Christian will get us to Duluth?" she asked aloud, not quite sure to whom the question was directed.

The letters on the necklace stirred around, producing a new word.

YES

"Ask it when," Torsten piped up from across the table.

The letters rolled—some closer to the surface, some floating off into the distance.

TOMORROW

FOUR PM

"Well, I guess that's that, then." Paivi watched the letters swirl back to their original places. She looked up hesitantly.

Paivi was surprised to see Mrs. Santos looking at her calmly.

"May I see it?" she asked, gesturing towards the locket.

"Oh, uh, sure." Paivi pulled it over her head and handed it to Mrs. Santos.

Mrs. Santos turned it over in her hands, admiring it.

"It's beautiful. My grandmother had one similar to

this."

Paivi looked at Mrs. Santos, shocked.

Jason stared at his mother, bewildered.

"Of course, hers wasn't in Gaelic, it was in Spanish. How does this one work?"

Paivi was confused. "I didn't know it did anything at all until it burned me tonight. And then the words started to move all over the surface. It turned into an alphabet soup and started sending us messages."

"Grandma told me she could send messages to people. Not letters or anything, but some other kind. She never really explained, but she always seemed to know if they were received or not." Mrs. Santos handed the locket back to Paivi.

Paivi pictured all of the messages she had gotten. Tater tots, cookies, sticks, signs along the road. She remembered seeing a chain around Christian's neck that disappeared under his shirt. That's how he had bothered her all those months. She wondered if he could look at her locket and see what else it was capable of.

"So, Mrs. Santos, your grandma was special, like my sister?" Torsten asked.

Paivi blushed and looked down at the locket in her hands. She had never told Jason about her abilities. She hoped he wouldn't see her as some kind of freak.

Jason still had a dazed look on his face. He listened, trying to grasp just what he was hearing.

"Oh, yes, grandma was special. I don't know what your talent is, Paivi, but she could move things, just by looking at them. She showed me once. It was wild! Her brother, Pépé, had a unique gift. He could speak any language in the world. He was like one of those electronic translators."

"Wait, slow down! Your grandma could move things with her mind?" Jason interrupted.

"That's nothing! Paivi blew out all the windows on our block before we left tonight." Torsten was excited to finally meet someone he could talk to about it.

Paivi was mortified and sank a little lower into her chair.

"Wow, that's impressive!" Mrs. Santos looked thoughtful. "No wonder you need to leave town. Grandma just showed me some small things, moving cups and spoons, things like that. She told me I had to promise not to tell anyone. My mother later told me that once there was an earthquake in grandma's village, when grandma was a young girl. Many of the houses collapsed, including the home of her aunt and uncle, who lived next door. They had three small children, my grandma's cousins, whom she loved dearly. The children were trapped under the collapsed walls and would have died if my grandma hadn't used her power to lift the walls and free them. She was only eleven at the time and didn't realize her gifts were special."

"She was able to save her cousins! That was a good thing," Jason said, as he focused intently on his mother's words.

"You would think so. But remember, grandma lived in a small village in Colombia. As far as the townspeople thought, talent like my grandma's was either a gift from God or a curse from the Devil. So they sent her to a convent until she was eighteen to ensure the townspeople thought it was no more than a miracle and she was spending her time thanking God for it."

"So why don't any of us have these abilities, Ma?" Jason asked.

"I'm not sure dear. As far as I know, the family gifts died with my grandma and her brother. My mother still has the necklace, the one that's similar to Paivi's. We'll have to have her show us sometime." Mrs. Santos got up from the table, clearing the glasses away. "It's getting late. You kids could all use some sleep, especially if you plan to travel tomorrow. Come on Jason, grab their backpacks and we can show them to the guest room."

Paivi and Torsten followed Jason and Mrs. Santos up the stairs to a small room on the second floor. There were two twin beds. The Santos' said goodnight and closed the door. No sooner did Paivi's head hit her pillow than she fell into a heavy sleep, her exhaustion finally catching up to her. She dreamt no dreams that night.

She woke to the smell of eggs and bacon. She pushed herself up onto one elbow, and fell back, groaning. Her muscles were sore and her face felt swollen and stiff.

"Are you awake?" She heard Torsten's voice across the room. He sounded hoarse.

"Yeah." Hers didn't sound much better.

"I'm starving and something smells good. Let's go

eat." Torsten rolled over, attempting to get up. "Ugh, everything hurts!"

They headed downstairs, entering the bright, sunny kitchen. The sun reflected off of the newly fallen snow. It was absolutely blinding if one looked at it too long.

Jason and his sister Jessica were already in the kitchen, preparing breakfast. Jason was stirring eggs in a pan on the stove, while Jessica loaded bread into the toaster.

"Good morning!" said Jessica brightly. "Have a seat—we're just about done here."

Paivi and Torsten took seats at the table, which had already been set for breakfast. Jason brought the pan of eggs to the table and Jessica arrived as well, carrying a plate each of toast and bacon.

"Ma!" Jessica shouted. "Breakfast is ready!"

They began passing the plates and the pan of eggs around, filling up their plates. Mrs. Santos joined them at the table, already dressed for the day.

"So, they told me what happened," said Jessica, as she spread jelly on her toast. "I hear you're leaving today?"

"Yeah, at four, I guess." Paivi picked up a forkful of eggs and took a dainty bite.

"I was thinking about it…since you are trying to travel 'incognito,' shall we say, that perhaps we should change your look."

"That's a great idea!" Torsten looked excited.

"What do we need to do?" asked Paivi.

"I'm thinking of giving you both a haircut and a different color. I'll run to the store after breakfast. I need a few supplies." Jessica took a bite of her toast. "Oh, we should make a list, too. You will probably need some things for your trip. I am going to guess you didn't have time to pack properly."

"You're right," Paivi said thoughtfully. She looked around the table. She didn't want to leave. The Santos' were so friendly—they made her feel almost normal. She just had to keep reminding herself that it wasn't possible. It wasn't safe.

After Jessica returned from the store with the necessary supplies, they got right to work. Torsten was up first. He suggested shaving off his dark, curly hair. Jason grabbed some clippers and Paivi and Jessica followed them down to the basement, where the laundry room became a makeshift hair salon. Jason finished clipping off the giant curls rather quickly. Jessica then stepped in, applying bleach to what was left of Torsten's hair, which wasn't much. He had to sit and wait for his hair to finish while they started on Paivi's new look. Jessica spritzed her hair with water and began snipping.

Paivi was glad there wasn't a mirror in the room. She knew the hair had to go, but she had quite liked her long, blond hair.

Oh well, she thought, *it's not like I can't have it that way again someday.*

Snip. Snip. Snip. Locks of blond hair were flying all over the place. Jason was attempting to keep it under control with a broom and dustpan, but was quickly losing the battle.

Paivi squeezed her eyes shut. She trusted Jessica not

to make her ugly.

"Okay, done." Jessica stepped back from her masterpiece. "Do you want to see?"

"Nope. I want to see the whole package, so show me after it's all finished," Paivi answered.

"Suit yourself!" Jessica began applying the hair dye. It was thick and cold. She massaged it through Paivi's hair like shampoo and piled what was left of her hair on top of her head. Jessica then led Torsten to the sink where she rinsed the dye out of his hair. The stubble on his head was light blond, almost white. He could've passed for Christian's brother.

Torsten ran down to the bathroom to inspect his new look in the mirror.

"Nice! I look tough!" Torsten stood up straight and folded his arms over his chest as he entered the laundry room.

"Sure you do!" laughed Jason. "And so does Beast!"

"Let's go Paivi, your turn to rinse." Jessica dragged her by the arm to the sink. "It's going to look great!"

Paivi leaned back in the chair, hanging her head into the laundry sink as Jessica rinsed the dye out. A quick shampoo and she was done. Jessica roughly dried her head with a towel and then quickly combed her hair. Out came the blow dryer and five minutes later, the masterpiece was complete.

Jason and Torsten admired the finished product while the hairdresser beamed at her handiwork.

"Wow, Jessica, it's amazing! I didn't know you were

such a talented hairdresser! Maybe you should think about dropping out of college and going to beauty school!" Jason said.

"Very funny. I can't help that I'm multi-talented. Don't be jealous!"

"Paivi, you look totally different. It's pretty cool!" Torsten added.

"That's it, I'm going to look!" Paivi jumped out of her chair and ran down to the bathroom. They were right—it was amazing. Her hair was cut into a short bob, falling just below her chin. A sweep of bangs fell across her forehead, nearly covering her left eye. The newly-dyed black hair accented her coloring, leaving her face looking like fine porcelain, with the exception of her battle scars from the previous night. Her eyes sparkled such a bright green that they looked unnatural. This was definitely not the old Paivi. No one would recognize her, which was exactly what she needed. For the first time in awhile, she smiled confidently at herself in the mirror.

They spent the remainder of the afternoon preparing to leave. Paivi and Torsten repacked their bags, adding in a few necessities that Jessica had picked up for them at the store. Mrs. Santos added a bag full of sandwiches and chips for the ride, as well as some bottles of water.

Promptly at four, a black SUV pulled up into the Santos' driveway. Jason went out to meet Christian, and had him pull the SUV into the garage. They had decided that it would be too dangerous to drive to Minnesota with Christian's original license plates. The Santos' had an old set of plates in the garage and Mrs. Santos felt it was best if they used them instead. Jason switched them quickly and they joined everyone in the warm kitchen.

Christian stood in the doorway, looking very uncomfortable. His face was more pale than usual, almost blending in with his white-blond hair. There were large dark rings under his eyes—he clearly had a rough night as well. He was fidgety, continually looking out the back door.

"Alright, we should get going. I've got maps in the car. I don't want to use any electronics, because everything can be traced these days. I understand we're heading north?" Christian nodded towards Paivi. "I got the message in my Cheerios."

"Yeah, Duluth. Hope you brought a heavy coat." Paivi began to put on her own coat, pulling up the zipper.

"Christian, you do have a license, don't you?" asked Mrs. Santos, her brow furrowed.

"Not quite. I was supposed to get it this month, but because of certain EOS policies, I was no longer allowed to get it," Christian answered. "But if it makes you feel better, I was the best driver in my class."

"Ma, seriously, his license doesn't matter anyways, right now he's not just driving illegally, he's pretty much living illegally. I'm thinking if he gets caught, the ATC won't be so concerned with the fact that he's driving without a license."

"Did they get your parents too, Christian?" Torsten asked.

"Yep, they came storming in around nine or so, right

before my parents went to bed. Dragged them out of the house in their pajamas, wouldn't even let them get their coat or shoes." Christian's eyes narrowed in anger, his hand gripped the chair in front of him, knuckles white.

"Oh, you poor kids! I just can't handle this. These ATC people are animals! How can they go around treating people like this! It's just not right. Are you sure you don't want us to go with you? I feel like we're abandoning you!" Mrs. Santos began to cry, tears sliding down her cheeks, and dropped into the nearest chair.

Paivi tried to fight back tears, but lost the battle. She looked around the room at the people who had showed so much love for her in such a short amount of time. She sniffed, wiping her eyes. It was time to go, before it got any more difficult.

"We should go. Thank you so much for everything. You really don't know how much this meant to us," Paivi said, trying to get the words out between tears. "We'll really miss you guys and we wish it was easier, and that we could just stay."

Mrs. Santos rose from her chair and walked around the table, holding first Paivi and then Torsten in a tight hug.

"Please call us if you need anything. And let us know you are okay, if you can," said Mrs. Santos between hugs. Christian even found himself on the receiving end of a hug, which he awkwardly accepted. Jessica made the rounds next, beginning to cry as well. Jason shook Torsten and Christian's hands, and Paivi and Torsten grabbed their bags as the group moved towards the back door to head to the car.

"Paivi, hold on a second." Jason pulled her back as everyone exited through the door. He gathered her into a big hug, holding her close. "I just want you to know that I love you, and I will miss you so much. I, uh, I ..."

He broke off, pressing his forehead to hers as tears sprang from his eyes. She cried harder and threw her arms around his neck. Seeing him cry made it all the worse. Through the tears, he pressed his lips to hers, a salty, bittersweet kiss.

"It's so unfair," he whispered through his tears.

"I have to go." Paivi pulled back from his embrace, but caught his hand, and led him out the back door. They ran across the yard to the garage, where Christian and Torsten had already claimed their spots in the car.

"Hey, who said you get shotgun?" Paivi punched Torsten in the arm as she climbed in the back seat.

"Ya snooze, ya lose, big sis. I called it, and you weren't out here," Torsten answered smugly.

"Goodbye and be safe!" pleaded Mrs. Santos one last time before the doors were shut.

The garage door opened and Christian pulled out, carefully making his way down the driveway. The Santos' waved a final farewell.

Christian maneuvered the car out onto the street and they made their way through St. Andrew as the early winter evening fell. They occasionally saw an ATC vehicle but they didn't have much to worry about—the streets were crowded with rush hour traffic. After about twenty minutes, they found themselves safely out of town without any problems and on the open road. They decided it was best to keep to the local roads, and stay off the interstate. Christian was concerned that there would be more ATC agents patrolling on the main roads. This route would take them longer, but they would come across less traffic and smaller towns, where the ATC weren't so concentrated.

They drove all night, passing through one farm town after the next, stopping at the occasional gas station to fill up or take a break. As they drove further north, the landscape grew in around them. Thick forests of birch trees closed in on the road on each side and it sometimes seemed like they were driving through a tunnel. Sometime after midnight, Paivi dozed off, the warmth of the car and the lull of the drive rocking her gently to sleep. She dreamed of Jason, they were holding hands and sitting close together on a beach. Palm trees swayed in the breeze. The sun shone brightly overhead and the sea lapped gently at their feet. She looked out over the scene in sadness—she knew this must be a dream, because it was near impossible that it was a vision of the future.

She awoke, finding herself in the SUV as it bumped over an uneven road. The sky was still dark, the stars and moon covered with clouds. There was no sun, no sea, no sand, no Jason. She sat back in the seat and sighed, looking out at the dark, snow covered forests that seemed to stretch on to infinity.

Chapter Twenty

The Road Less Taken

In the early light of dawn, Paivi could see the bridges across Lake Superior that would take them from Wisconsin to Minnesota. The clouds had cleared and it looked to be a sunny day. This was quite deceiving, as the air here was far colder than it had been in St. Andrew. Paivi wished she had a blanket, as the SUV had become increasingly cold, despite the fact that the heater was turned all the way up.

Paivi was surprised that she remembered where Tim and Alissa lived. She had only been to their house once, about two years ago. Tim was her dad's cousin, and he and his wife and daughter, Monika, had come to visit them in St. Andrew many times throughout her childhood. They wound their way through the hilly streets. Little San Francisco, as Duluth was sometimes called; it was not far from the truth. Turning right on Seventh Street, Christian slowed down.

"I don't want to just drive up to this house. What if it's not safe? I think we should drive past and see what we have going on here. Maybe we should even park the car one block over and walk up, just in case we have to run for it,"

Christian suggested.

"That's fine. There it is. 680 Seventh Street." Paivi pointed to a small, white, one-story house to their left.

Christian slowed down, allowing them to have a look. The house and lawn were covered with a foot of white snow. There were two trucks in the driveway. Steam billowed from the furnace vent in the roof. Somebody was living there, at least. As they passed, they could hardly help but notice as the Christmas lights in the widows rearranged themselves to read one word.

SAFE

"Whoa, did you see that?" Torsten was bewildered. "Did those lights seriously just move or am I going crazy?"

"They moved. Remember, it's like mom and dad said, special people will sometimes mark their houses, so others like them will know that they are there. I am guessing they didn't generally use the words 'safe' before," Paivi said.

"Yeah, I guess I shouldn't be so surprised, right? In the past two days I've seen my sister blow the windows out of every house in the neighborhood and listened to a necklace that is sending us messages in some kind of crazy alphabet soup."

Christian turned right, and pulled a little further up the street before parking the SUV.

"Let's just leave our things here for right now. If we bring bags, it may look suspicious," Christian suggested.

They opened the doors and were hit with the bitingly cold air as it slapped them in the face. If Paivi had been cold in the car, she was freezing to near death now. The snow was deep and the sidewalks were not plowed, so they chose to walk along the side of the street. They kept their eyes peeled the entire way. They hadn't seen any ATC agents since entering Duluth, but they knew they had to be here somewhere. Maybe it was just too early and the ATC knew no one would dare be out at such an hour in the cold.

The driveway at 680 Seventh Street had been plowed and the sidewalk shoveled. They edged slowly up the drive, past the trucks to the front door. Paivi took a deep breath and knocked lightly.

"You have to knock harder than that! No one is going to hear that light tap." Christian knocked harder on the door.

Paivi gulped. This was it. Either the necklace was right and they had come to the right place, or someone else lived here and they were stuck, in frozen Duluth, Minnesota, with nowhere to go. What would they do next? Paivi's mind was racing over the possibilities. Maybe they could go back to St. Andrew and hide in Jason's basement.

The door opened, bringing Paivi back to reality. A short woman with long, blond hair opened the door just a crack.

"Can I help you?" She sounded nervous.

"Um, Alissa, do you remember me?" Paivi was even more nervous.

Alissa lifted her eyes to look more closely at the three strangers on her doorstep.

"I'm sorry, I don't."

Paivi could feel tension radiating from the boys

behind her.

"It's Paivi, my dad is John."

"Paivi? Oh my god, I didn't recognize you! Who is with you?" She glanced at the boys.

"Oh, my brother, Torsten and my friend Christian."

"Okay, quick, come inside. You guys are so grown up! Torsten, you look like you're twenty-five! Did you happen to see any ATC agents around?" Alissa quickly shut the door behind them and locked two deadbolts.

"No, none."

"Phew. They've been hanging around the neighborhood lately. Tim is getting nervous that they are on to us." She ushered them into the kitchen.

The house smelled like cinnamon, it reminded Paivi of home. She looked around and saw pictures of the family on the mantel of the small brick fireplace. Pictures of Monika involved in various activities hung on the walls. The rooms she could see were small but cozy.

"Please, sit down, make yourselves comfortable. Would you care for something to drink? Something warm?" Alissa offered.

"That would be awesome! It's freezing here!" Torsten replied.

"How about some hot cocoa—I think I have some marshmallows in here somewhere." She disappeared into the pantry.

"That sounds great." Torsten smiled nervously at Paivi.

"So, what brings you here? I'm guessing something

happened at home, or you wouldn't be showing up on my doorstep so early on a Monday morning without your Mom and Dad."

"Our parents are gone. They took them." Paivi felt she didn't even need to say the name anymore. Everyone in the room knew whom she meant.

Alissa passed steaming, hot mugs to them from the stove. She brought the bag of marshmallows to the table and took the last empty seat.

"I'm not surprised. I heard they rounded up a couple down the street last night as well. One of the neighbors called to let us know." She rested her chin on her fist.

Paivi noticed something. Or rather, noticed something was missing. She didn't notice an EOS sign in the front yard, and she didn't see any EOS badges recharging in the house.

"They don't know about you!" she blurted out, too tired to think about whether it was something to discuss or not.

"Pardon?" Alissa looked nervous again.

Paivi was nervous too. She looked around. Maybe this was some kind of trap.

"They don't know about you. You don't have a sign in your yard and you don't have any EOS badges. How did you manage that? Are you going to turn us in?" Paivi started to push her chair back, tense, prepared to run. The boys eyed her nervously.

"Wait, please, just listen," she pleaded, hands raised. "I promise, we won't turn you in. We would never do such a thing. We've been helping EOS people, people like you."

"Well, how is it that you have your Christmas lights spelling out words in the window, but you don't have an EOS badge." Paivi asked.

"We aren't sure. For some reason, we were left off the list, and no one ever turned us in, if they knew. So we've been sort of running a safe house. A week ago, we helped a few people go north, over the border into Canada. We've had a few people ask for our help since then. So we put the sign in the window, but it's only meant for people who are looking to truly be safe. The ATC can't see it, even if they have someone like us working for them, which is unlikely, there aren't so many of us up here."

Paivi's locket started to heat up, but she didn't feel comfortable looking at it. She touched it and met Christian's eye. She hoped the locket would hurry up and cool down.

"So what about us? Can you help us get to Canada?" Christian asked, stirring marshmallows into his cocoa.

The locket cooled significantly.

"Well, we'll have to see what Tim says when he gets up. You guys are family, not like the other people he took north. I mean, I think it's safe, we would never take people somewhere dangerous, but you guys are just kids."

"Just kids who drove eight hours from St. Andrew and have managed to not get caught by the ATC," Christian reminded her.

"Good point," she chuckled at his bravado. "Why don't I make some pancakes? Are you guys hungry?"

"Pancakes sound really good. Thanks," said Paivi,

finally removing her coat and hanging it on the back of the chair.

While Alissa cooked, she kept them preoccupied with small talk, asking how their parents had been doing, telling them all about Monika and her many athletic talents, and discussing the weather.

"It's been a warm winter, you're lucky!" said Alissa, bringing a plate of steaming hot pancakes to the table.

"Warm? You call this warm? This is like being at the North Pole! I figured we'd see Santa Claus walking down the street here!" laughed Torsten. "I am surprised the lake isn't frozen, I figured we could just like, skip the bridge and drive right across!"

"Funny! Today is a little colder than it has been. We've been pretty lucky though, winter is usually a lot colder by this time. But Lake Superior doesn't freeze over any more. I think it used to, but only every twenty years or so. Now, with global warming, it doesn't even partially freeze until January or February. It would be cool though, to be able to drive across the lake!"

There was a noise from the hallway, and a tall man with blond hair entered the room, looking slightly surprised.

"Well, hello. I didn't know you were expecting company so early." The man moved towards Alissa.

"Tim, you remember your cousin John's kids, Paivi and Torsten? And this is their friend Christian. Their parents are gone."

His face rose and then fell.

"Paivi, Torsten, I wouldn't have recognized you! I

am happy to see you, but sorry it has to be under such circumstances." He walked around the table, giving them each a big hug. "Nice to meet you, Christian." He shook Christian's hand heartily.

"Our parents told us they were going to call you, to see if we could come here. They didn't want us to stay in St. Andrew anymore; it was getting bad. It was the last thing we talked about before they were taken." Paivi sighed. "So coming to Duluth was the only thing we could think of."

"Well, you made the right decision. I can't believe you made it all the way here without getting caught. That's impressive. But I've heard the ATC is much more active in the major cities and the suburbs. We have only a small group here, but unfortunately they've been snooping around, so it's a bit scary."

"So, Tim, what do you think? Alissa was mentioning to us that you took some people to Canada. Do you think we should go there?" Paivi asked.

"Well, I certainly think it's safer for you to go there than to stay here, especially with the ATC sniffing around. But I don't know, it might be too late to make the trip." He looked thoughtful.

"Tim, they're so young! Would it be safe?" Alissa sounded worried.

"It's not easy, but it's not completely unsafe." He looked them over. "They look like they could handle it. They're pretty athletic."

Tim filled a plate with pancakes and dragged an extra chair over to the table. He sat down and poured syrup over the top of the small stack. He cut them and put a forkful into his mouth.

"Now that's good stuff. All right, so you have a car with you? And some bags or something?"

"Yeah, we parked the car up a side street," Christian answered, "and our bags are in the back."

"Okay, so here's what we'll do. I have a friend with some property, like fifty acres, about twenty minutes outside of Duluth. We'll take the truck there and hide it, he won't mind. Then we will put your bags in the back of our truck and drive back. It's best if you wait here, though, it's not safe for you guys to be out and about."

"You're going to take my truck?" Christian seemed surprised by the suggestion.

"Well, I don't suppose you want them tracing the license plates and realizing you're somewhere in the neighborhood. Like I said, they are already poking around here. We don't want to give them any reason to start going door-to-door checking papers."

"Okay. I understand." Christian relented.

"After breakfast here I will make a few calls to see if it's possible to still get to Canada. There are some other options if that won't work, but it will take a little more planning in order to get you where you've got to go. If it's possible, you may be leaving tonight."

"Tonight!" Paivi squeaked. "That just seems so fast!"

"Yeah, well, it's not a vacation, and the sooner you guys are out of here, the better it is for all of us. If we have a bunch of people staying here for long periods, they'll bust us for sure." Tim looked serious.

Paivi played with her last few pieces of pancake. She thought about crying. But why? What good would it do? They needed to leave, the locket said to run, and it told them to go north. It didn't necessarily say to stop at Duluth. It heated up every time they mentioned Canada, and if she could look at it, she was sure it would say to keep going. They would be safe there. It is what she begged her parents to do. If only they could be there with them. But they weren't. Instead, she and Torsten were all alone, without papers—illegal and depending on others to help them. She gathered herself together.

"Okay. We'll be ready for whatever." Paivi looked confidently at Torsten, who looked a bit nervous at the thought of such an early departure as well. "What will we do once we get to Canada?"

"If I can take you to the same place, there is a house where other people like us are staying. I am not sure what will happen once you get there. But I know they will help you. A lot of this is word of mouth, so we are just trusting you'll be in good hands. Regardless, you will be in Canada and you will be free of the ATC. You may just have to deal with the Canadian government, but I'd take them any day over the ATC. If the Canadians catch you though, be sure to claim political asylum. Tell them your story. It's the only way to keep them from sending you back, because they will have to investigate, and most likely, you would get it. You're just kids. I can't imagine that they would deny kids political asylum."

Alissa came around to pick up their plates. They rose to help her clear the table.

"I'm going to wake up Monika and have her come down. I'm sure she'd love to see you guys before you go. Then we'll get going and move the truck." Alissa headed down the hall.

"Feel free to take a shower or take a nap while we are gone. It could be a long night," Tim suggested.

Paivi, Torsten and Christian moved to the living room, settling into the couch and flipping on the television. Torsten, tired and full of pancakes, fell asleep right away, snoring because he was sleeping while sitting up on the couch. His head hung back, mouth wide open.

Tim and Alissa made their way to the front door, zipping up their coats and pulling on boots.

"We'll need the keys. What kind of car is it?" Tim asked, walking towards the couch.

"Black SUV. Illinois plates. It's just around the corner. You can't miss it." Christian pulled a key off of a key ring and handed it to Tim.

Tim and Alissa opened the door and with a blast of cold air, walked out into the sunny morning.

Paivi looked at him funny. "Why didn't you just give him the whole key ring?"

"Well, he can keep the car key. But these are my house keys. Maybe I'll need them... someday." Christian sounded wistful.

"Do you really think we're coming back?" she

asked.

"I don't know. Sometimes I hope so. Sometimes I never want to see this place again. But you know it depends on whether I get to see my parents again. I can only imagine what they're going through. I'll let them decide where we should live." Christian sounded sad for the first time.

"Are we doing the right thing, leaving? My dad kept telling me only cowards and guilty people would run." Paivi played with the zipper on her sweatshirt, thinking back to the image of her mother in the camp. She didn't have to imagine what their parents were going through. She's seen it.

"Where's your dad now? What choice did we have? Just sit around the house and wait for them to pick us up? You know they wouldn't have let us stay there for long. I don't understand why they didn't just take us all at once. Maybe it's easier for them to keep us away from our parents or something. I bet the ATC didn't think we'd run. I wonder if anyone else did."

The day dragged slowly by. Christian didn't feel comfortable not having someone on watch while Alissa and Tim were gone, so he and Paivi took turns sleeping and watching out the front window. Torsten continued to snore into the afternoon. Monika joined them in the living room.

"So, my Mom said you are just visiting for the day because you are on vacation. That's cool! Where are you going next?" she asked.

"Oh, Christian has some relatives in another part of Minnesota that we are going to visit for, uh, Christmas," Paivi answered, noticing the small Christmas tree in the corner. She felt Monika was too young to hear the truth.

"Is Christian your boyfriend?" Monika asked.

Christian heard the question, even though he was supposed to be napping. Paivi saw his mouth turn up into a smile.

"Um, no. Christian is just a friend. He told us he was going to have to drive here alone, and we felt sorry for him. My parents were going, uh…out of town, so we were going to be on our own anyways."

"Oh, cool. Want to make some bracelets with me?" Monika hauled out a huge box of beads and thread from under the coffee table. "I've got to make a few more for Christmas presents."

Paivi was glad of the distraction, and spent the better part of the afternoon stringing beads with Monika. She couldn't sleep anyways.

Tim and Alissa returned at dinnertime carrying some plastic bags.

"We brought dinner, we knew there wouldn't be much time to cook." Alissa lifted the lid off a cardboard bucket.

Paivi's mouth started to water as the smell of fried chicken filled the room.

"Um, how did everything go?" Paivi asked nervously.

Tim glanced at Monika. "I talked to my friend. It seems that we will be able to go out later. We'll get ready after we eat."

The meal was a quick one, chicken and small tubs of

mashed potatoes and gravy were passed around the table. Paivi forgot she hadn't eaten since breakfast and that she was starving. Torsten had almost an entire chicken on his plate. He certainly hadn't lost his appetite. After dinner, Alissa ushered Monika down the hall, encouraging her to get ready for bed and promising to watch a movie with her later.

Tim addressed Paivi, Torsten and Christian.

"Okay. So we will leave in an hour. Your bags are already in the truck. We took the plates off the SUV and hid them in a forest on the way back. We also scratched off the VIN number, in case they find it. It will just look like some car thieves ditched it there, which happens from time to time. We are going to drive about thirty minutes north of Duluth, along the lakefront. There is a park there with a boat landing that's popular with fisherman. I have a friend with a fishing boat that he stores there. He can get it in the water pretty quickly, being that it hasn't frozen along the coast yet. We'll go north along the coast to just over the Canadian border, and leave you at the drop off point. Someone is supposed to meet you there and take you to the cabin in the woods. There are no roads or anything where we're taking you, so it's important that they meet you or you could get lost and freeze to death. Make sure to put on as many heavy clothing items as you can, a couple shirts, two or three pairs of socks, whatever you can manage. You're going to need the insulation out in that cold."

They washed up quickly and dressed themselves with all the layers they had brought inside. Tim had to bring in their bags so they could find a few more pairs of socks.

Finally, it was time.

Monika and Alissa came out to say goodbye.

"Are you sure you don't want to stay for the movie?" Monika asked, balancing a giant bowl of popcorn.

"We'd love to, but we've got to get going! But thanks! Enjoy the movie!" Paivi gave Monika a big hug. She moved on to Alissa. "Thanks for everything."

Alissa hugged her. "Good luck."

They pulled on their winter coats over their thick layers of clothing. Paivi felt a little warm, but knew it would be worth it once they stepped outside.

The cold hit them as they headed out the door. Paivi started to shiver and tried to force herself to stop. There was no use shivering yet, she had a feeling it was going to get a whole lot worse as the night went on.

The drive to the park was quiet. Paivi was busy looking out at the woods, thinking about having to walk alone through them in the dark, while Christian continued to keep an eye out for any ATC vehicles.

They followed a winding two-lane road along the coast. It was the most major road in these parts, being that it was actually paved, and yet there was very little traffic. A half an hour after leaving the house, they pulled off the road onto a snow-covered side road that Paivi would have driven right by. It was barely a hole in a wall of trees, slightly bigger than the truck itself. Tim eased the truck down the road to a clearing, where another truck waited with a small fishing boat on a trailer. Tim got out and ran over to the other driver. The other man maneuvered his truck around angling the trailer towards an opening that Paivi could see led out to the black water. She noticed for the first time that she could see the moon and stars tonight. The moon wasn't full, but it reflected off of the water, making it appear much brighter. She could see so many stars out of the window of the truck that she felt like she was in a planetarium.

Tim returned quickly and told them to grab their belongings. Paivi pulled on her backpack and opened the truck door. She didn't think it was possible to be colder than cold, but this was colder than she could ever imagine was even possible.

"Don wants us to throw everything in the boat before we put it in the water. Once it's in we'll have you guys hop on board. We'll come on last, we'll have to push the boat out a few feet, but we have waders so we'll stay dry." He grabbed what appeared to be a pair of rubber overalls and began to step into them. "We use these for fishing, but they come in handy for launching a boat in the winter, too!"

Paivi, Torsten and Christian stayed close together for warmth as they moved down the clearing towards the boat. They threw their bags over the side and stepped out of the way as Don backed the truck in so that the trailer and the boat were in the water. Tim grabbed a rope and pushed the boat back into the lake. He gave a wave to the truck, which accelerated forward, pulling the trailer back out of the water. Paivi could see the water freezing instantly, forming little icicles on it. Don parked the truck and then headed back to the boat to help everyone on.

INTO THE SHADOWS

Christian went first, taking a step up on Don and Tim's hands. Paivi went next, pulling herself over the side of the boat with Christian's help. She slipped on the deck and fell just as Torsten came over the top rail, landing in a heap on top of her.

"Ow, you idiot!" she whispered at him loudly, not wanting to make a lot of noise although it didn't appear that there were any humans anywhere nearby.

"I didn't know you we're going to be here. Come on, let's get out of the way." Torsten half dragged her down the deck to the back of the boat.

Tim and Don joined them after helping push the boat out a little further. They made their way to the back of the boat and Don climbed up a small ladder to the captain's deck. There was an enclosed area with room for three people and the controls. "Hi kids, nice to meet ya. Tim and I are going to be up on the captain's deck, so we'll have to put you down below in the cabin. The ride is going to last for a few hours, and the heater isn't much, but it'll keep us all from freezing to death. Don't come up on deck until we come down to get you, it's too slippery and we don't want any of you falling overboard. Once you fall into that," he nodded towards the black water, "there's very little chance we will find you alive."

Paivi shivered as she looked out over the dark water. Escaping the country was definitely scary, but not nearly as scary as that great stretch of blackness that could swallow them into a grave that no one would ever find. She happily followed the others below deck into the small cabin. She didn't even mind that it smelled like fish. At least it was warm. The room was decorated with pictures of fish and beer advertisements. It had a small kitchen area and a couch that had the ability of transforming into a bed. They dropped their bags into a corner and settled into the couch as Don headed for the door.

"Bon voyage kids. There's a little phone over to the side there if you need to call up to us. You'll need to keep the lights off in order to keep us from being seen from the shore. You can use the flashlights over in the corner if you'd like a little light. Just keep it away from the windows. See you in a bit." He flicked the lights off and shut the door tight.

Paivi sat in the middle, crammed between Torsten and Christian. That was fine, it meant that she was warmer than either of them. Her eyes attempted to adjust to the dark, but she couldn't make out a thing, not even her hand before her face. She reached behind her and felt a curtain hanging over a window and pushed it to the side. A little light came through from the moonlight reflecting off the water. At least she could make out some objects around the room.

"What do we do now?" Paivi sighed.

"I've got some cards, if you want to play," Torsten offered.

"Um, if you haven't noticed, it's a little dark. How are we supposed to play cards?" Paivi retorted.

"Well, he said we could use the flashlights." He pulled the pack of cards out of his pocket.

"Come on Torsten." Christian got up, grabbing one of the flashlights. "I'll play with you."

After a half an hour attempting to play hearts in the light of a dim flashlight, the boys gave up, returning to plop down on the couch next to Paivi.

"Now what?" Torsten asked.

Paivi was suffering from the incessant rocking of the boat, her stomach rolled back and forth and her head spun.

"I don't know what you're gonna do, but I feel sick. All I want to do is close my eyes and sleep." She closed her eyes, hoping the rocking motion would subside. It helped.

Torsten and Christian were quiet, and soon Torsten was snoring, as usual. Paivi didn't dare open her eyes to see if Christian was sleeping or not. She didn't feel like talking anyways. Soon, her exhaustion got the better of her and she drifted off to sleep, leaning against Torsten. She awoke to feel someone pulling on her arm.

"Paivi, Torsten, wake up. We're here." It was Christian. He was shaking them both now. "Come on, we've got to be ready to go. They are pulling us into shore."

Paivi looked around her. Everything was so dark—it took her a few seconds to realize where they were. Now she remembered. They were on a boat on Lake Superior in the middle of the night, attempting to escape to Canada. Then she remembered the cold. She sat up. She looked at Torsten who was rubbing the sleep from his eyes and Christian, who was putting on his backpack. She didn't want to go outside, it was too cold!

Tim appeared in the doorway. "Don is just about to pull up to the shore. Are you guys ready?"

Paivi felt sick, and she wasn't sure if it was from the

seasickness or from nerves. She grabbed her backpack, slipping it on.

"We're ready."

"Be careful on the deck, it's extremely slippery," Tim warned.

They followed him out onto the deck. The air felt colder here, maybe more so because this was the end of the line. They were on their own from here. No more friends to help them. Just the cold, dark woods stretching out in front of them. Paivi looked out over the lake—it looked beautiful in the night. The silver light of the moon spread across the black surface giving it the appearance liquid mercury. Don came down from the captain's deck and helped them move to the front of the boat.

"How did you guys know where to take us?" Torsten asked.

"You'll see when you get to the front of the boat," Tim answered.

Slipping and sliding, they cautiously made their way to the front of the boat. Along the shoreline, Paivi could see the trees. Instead of forming a straight wall, they were bent into awkward shapes that took her a minute to understand. The trees were shaped into a word.

SAFE

Before their eyes, there was a slight rustle and the trees moved back to their original positions. Paivi had never seen a sign on such a scale. It was amazing. She wondered if Don could see it, but she didn't think it was important.

"Okay, let's have the boys jump first, then you guys

can catch Paivi. If I remember, she was always the clumsy one." Tim pointed to the edge of the boat.

"Very funny," Paivi said through chattering teeth.

Christian went over first, with a light splash as he landed in the water. Torsten followed with a splash of his own.

"Now quick, hop down so they don't have to stand in that water any longer, it's only like a few inches, but you guys don't need any extra water on you in this cold."

Paivi swung her legs over the bar and hopped down a few feet into the shallow water, Torsten and Christian catching her arms so she didn't lose her balance. With her luck she would have fallen face first into the water and then froze to death. They moved quickly to the shore.

"Now, someone is supposed to meet you here." Tim looked up and down the shore, squinting to see if he could spot someone in the trees. "I don't want to leave you kids here alone."

Paivi looked around. The shore looked so familiar. She stepped to the side, away from the boat and looked back out at the lake. She closed her eyes a moment and it hit her like a ton of bricks. She had been here before. "I think you should go. We don't want you guys to get caught."

"Paivi, are you crazy? If they leave us here and we don't get to this house or whatever is supposedly out there in the woods, we'll freeze to death!" Christian sputtered.

She gave him a dirty look. "I wouldn't tell them to leave if I thought we were going to freeze to death. This is the right place."

Don looked nervous—he kept scanning the shoreline as well. "I think she's right, Tim, we better go. We've got to try to get back to the landing before daylight."

"Alright. Good luck you guys. I hope to see you all again soon. Send us a message when you get a chance." Tim waved to them.

Don and Tim moved to the back of the boat and climbed up to the captain's deck. The engine started and the boat backed slowly away from the shore. It began moving out into the night, following the silver path until it disappeared from their view.

Paivi took a deep breath, which was difficult in the cold air. It burned in her lungs and nose. She looked at the water one last time and then turned towards the tall quiet wall of trees.

"Now what are we going to do?" asked Torsten, looking nervously up and down the shoreline.

"I know where to go." Paivi smiled and pulled up her scarf. "Follow me."

She took a step into the shadows and closed her eyes. She let her feet lead the way, just as they had in her vision. Torsten and Christian fell in step behind her. One by one they disappeared into the dark forest. The locket began to heat up under her clothes, she was thankful not only for it's warmth but also it's guidance. She knew the heat meant they were getting close. The snow was deep, up to their knees, slowing their progress. Paivi pressed on, eager to get them to safety.

"Are we there yet?" whined Torsten through

chattering teeth.

"Almost," Paivi responded. She could see a hint of light ahead.

The trees abruptly ended at a clearing. Before them stood a log cabin, with warmth and light spilling from the frosty windowpanes. A wisp of smoke trailed from the chimney. They had made it. This was the next step towards their future safe from the ATC, EOS badges and harassment.

"Now what?" asked Christian quietly.

"Come on!" Paivi grabbed them both by the arms and led them to the front porch. She raised her hand to knock on the front door and before she could even touch it, it flew open. An old woman stood in the bright doorway.

"Welcome! We've been waiting for you," she said, offering a warm smile.

Paivi smiled back and stepped into the light.

Acknowledgments

It is misleading that only my name is on the cover of this book, because as all writers know, it takes more than one person to write a book. There are countless people who have had a hand in this book in some way, and it would take me pages to thank them all. I'll try my best to fit them all on this page.

First and foremost, I would like to thank my daughter, Annikka Päivi. She was my inspiration in so many ways and continues to keep me moving forward every day. I have to thank my husband, Richard, who has always supported me 100% and sacrificed his time and energy to help me in every way he could. Thanks to my parents, Mike and Vicki, for introducing me to books and always encouraging my wild imagination. They help me in so many millions of ways. Thanks to my brother, Michael, for sharing the dream, and the rest of our family for their interest and support.

I have a million cheerleaders, to whom I am grateful every day, because they believe in me, even on days I don't believe in myself (and put up with my rambling about writing!). Thanks and hugs to my friends, Timmy Olson, Sue Rendall, Stacy and Tom Diederich, Stephanie and Chad Kelly, Kelly and Ben Rakow, Weston, and Lee and Rachel Saldaña. Many thanks to all my Facebook friends, Twitter friends, and blog followers for their kind words and encouragement.

I also have to mention my cheerleaders at Schaumburg High School, Jen Langer, Kate Haskins, Kelly Kennedy, Greg Charvat, Sara Dopke, Cindy Arroyo, and Darrell Robin. And of course I can't forget my students. It would be so much harder to write stories if I didn't have the living, breathing characters standing right in front of me every day. Their energy and enthusiasm makes all the difference! Thanks to all of my current German and French students at Schaumburg High, including those from the best German 2 class in 2009 (home of the giant, fat, flying cat), and all of my former students from both Schaumburg and Palatine High. You guys make this so much more exciting!

And finally, I have to mention my writer-friends. These people have given me invaluable advice and support, and they are truly the reason I am a better writer. Michelle Sussman, Sarah Barthel, and Natalie Rompella are just the tip of the SCBWI iceberg. I don't know what I'd do without you. And though I've never had the honor of meeting him (I hope to someday), I have to thank ebook master, Joe Konrath. Without the expertise that he shares with the world, this process would have been so much more difficult and scary.

Thanks to you, the reader, for giving me a chance.

I think that covers everyone, but if you feel I've forgotten you, I owe you a hug and a big THANKS!

INTO THE SHADOWS

Special Thanks To: Maria English, Tina Davies-Crompton, Rose Sengenberger, Michael Hartsfield, Dorothy Dreyer, Ardith Richter, Thomas Fortenberry, Simeren Mago Silverstein, Jake Sniffer, Alicia Kerner, Karisa Turek LaFleur, Jane Froud, Jen Turner, Michelle Sussman, Chris Whigham, Christian Gustafson, Bret Praxmarer, Koko Love Summer (Anthony Bruno), Laura Crawford, Kirsten Bergstrom, Aimee Kasel-Weber, Cassandra Fox, Lauren Gibson McDonald, Timmy Olson, Kelly Forkell Rakow, Brian Pettera, Matt Wehmeier, Author Zulmara, Ashlynn Monroe, Nicky Jacobs, Natalie Rompella, Colleen Rowan Kosinski, D.B. Grady, Jeanie Brew, Lou Riddell, Cat Toerber, Keith Mohr, Amanda Heroman, Linda Govik, John Kennedy, Traci Leigh Milligan, Cherie Colyer, Adrienne Crezo, Lindsey Sullivan Brandner, Stepanie Mock Kelly, Rachel Shannon Saldaña, Ben Rakaow, Leevell Saldaña, Matt Weston, Angela Cardinal, Patti Domain-Bryant, Sue Ellen Rendall, Edward Domain, Marlene Deckert, Michael Kirkpatrick (Dad), Michael Kirkpatrick (bro), Vicky Hernandez, Vicki Kirkpatrick, Jennifer Klor Langer, Darshanandini 'Dolly' Napal, Chad Kelly, Jean Domain, Shnea Biggins, Antoine Townsend, Kate Evon Haskins, Samantha Rill, Talli Roland, Shonell Bacon, Danielle Tauscher, Alma Sabic, Amber McCoy, Gary House, Marcel Bondarowicz, Kelsey Townley, Matt W. Bolger, Morgan Bolger, Aaron Borst, Sam Serafin, Jim Wehmeier, Daniel Skiroock, Dean Serafin, Cintya Mejia, Will Lucnik, Ben Broeski, Kedar Mehra, Jalen Little, Katie Leigh, Sammi Packard, Lexi Awdziejczyk, Zoe Zuleger, Sori Gim, Ethan

Miller, Nataline Shakro, Melina Reynoso, Brian Greszkowiak, Jocquil Givens, Bianka Guajardo, Samantha McKeown, Leili Mashhadi, Ali Rizzo, Katey Bergstrom, Allie Long, Ema Cigerova, Ervin Vega, Murray Barrus, Maika Kumamoto, Jason Cokkinias, Matthew Jablenski, Shaun McGuire, Zijo Zulic, Sanjin Ibrahimovic, Christopher Rion, Jocelynn Kim, Jen Niewinski, Krista Legan, Rebecca Whitehead, Julie Friedberg, Natasha Alley, Jason Brescia, Mike Scully, Patrick Jost, Brittany Tamason, John Badziong, Cameron Popek, Lisa Ciurca Miles, Jenner Fulton, Rich Steeves, Hayden Black, Terence Cumberworth, Jeffrey Getzin, Cristina Hernandez, Jen Springborn, Sara Callahan Balgeman, Carl Graves, Rob Siders, Krista Goldie, and Elena Martina

Karly Kirkpatrick is a YA writer, avid reader, high school German and French teacher, and mother of a toddler. She is currently pursuing an MA in Writing and Publishing at DePaul University in Chicago. She lives in Elgin, Illinois with her husband, daughter, and two stinky Shih Tzus. To contact Karly, read her blog, or find out about upcoming releases, go to www.karlykirkpatrick.com.